Eve Adams lives in Surrey, and 2000 will
see her three new books published. Two
fairytales for children, *Christmas Eve* and
The Reluctant Fairy Godfather, are now
joined by *Twisting Tails.* This is a collection
of fourteen original short stories with, as
the title suggests, a twist in each tail.

TWISTING TAILS

BY
EVE ADAMS

With best wishes
in your new
job,

Eve Adams
December 3
2024

**EV
BOOKS**

Published and Distributed by E. V. Books
3 Canada Road, Byfleet, Surrey KT14 7JL.

FIRST EDITION

First Published August 2000

© by E. V. Books 2000
© Cover Illustration by T K Spencer

ISBN 0-9538369-2-4

Set in Times 11 on 12pt.
Design and Typesetting by
T K Art & Design, Addlestone, Surrey.

Printed in Great Britain by
Woking Print & Publicity
Woking, Surrey.

For Richard, Jon and Kerri
With Love

CONTENTS

METAMORPHOSIS

As far back as she could remember she had wanted to be beautiful. The plain dumpy child had grown into a plain dumpy woman. No amount of dieting could counteract the eating binges; as fast as she lost a couple of pounds she would put them back on with her compulsive snack attacks. At the age of 23 she had already given up the struggle, resigned to living her life as a fat frump.

She had a sweet nature and was a popular young lady, but any hopes she might have had of finding a man to love and take care of her had faded long ago. Prone to outbreaks of spots due to her poor diet, and noticeably overweight, she seemed to be caught in a vicious circle. Trying to lose the excess pounds made her miserable, so she ate more and more bars of chocolate in an attempt to cheer herself up.

Depression was a regular companion, but she put a brave face on things and got on with her life. Lonely and unhappy with her looks, she threw herself into her work to fill as many hours of each day as possible, and was regarded as a reliable, efficient member of staff.

The crunch had come at an office party three months ago. She had had a crush on the Sales Manager since he had come to work with the company the year before, but he always had a pretty woman on his arm. She had learned to adore him from afar, trying not to show her feelings when he was around.

The party was in full swing when he came over to her and offered her a drink. She gazed up at him, her heart pounding as he stood close to her.

'Such a handsome man,' she thought, trying not to

stammer as she accepted the proffered glass of wine. He had flashed her that knockout smile of his, and her knees had gone weak.

As he turned to walk away she heard him say over his shoulder, 'Enjoy yourself, Chubs.' She had frozen, her smile rigid at the sound of her hated nickname, not meant to hurt but devastatingly painful from his lips.

She was mortified. She watched him cross the room and put his arm around the shoulders of the prettiest girl at the party as she stood rooted to the spot with shame, her cheeks bright red and her stomach churning.

Her heart sinking, she fled to the ladies' cloakroom as the tears came. That night she lay on her bed sobbing miserably. She picked up a magazine to take her mind off her woes and became absorbed in an article about plastic surgery, something that had crossed her mind once or twice before.

She read about a clinic in London which had recently opened. The surgeons there were using the latest technology to alter their clients' faces and bodies, and she drifted off to sleep determined to book an appointment to see one of the consultants as soon as possible.

The receptionist at the clinic had been extremely helpful over the phone, and she had plucked up her courage and made her first appointment to see one of the cosmetic surgeons working there.

During the previous weeks she had seen Mr. Parker twice. An extremely affable man, he had put her mind at ease at once, assuring her that he could help her with her problems in a very short space of time. Friendly and easy-going, he had discussed everything with her and convinced her that she would be safe in his hands. She liked him very much, and knew instinctively that she could trust him to do his very best for her.

He had put her on a strict diet which she had struggled

with, but her determination to succeed had seen her lose 18 pounds very quickly. Her confidence began to increase, the surgery was booked, and now here she was - lying in her hospital bed with light bandages covering her face, the operation successfully over.

She had taken Mr. Parker's advice as to what changes she should go for, and he had completed the 'renovation' as she liked to call it. She would be in the clinic for only two days, followed by a week at home while the bruising died down.

Her eyes and nose had been re-sculpted, and she had undergone a facial laser peel, which would improve the texture of her skin remarkably. In the taxi home from the clinic she was in very little discomfort, just a twinge now and then, but overall she was thrilled to have the surgery behind her, and a new life ahead of her.

She had taken two weeks' holiday from the company but had told no-one where she would be. Dosing herself with arnica to help with the bruising, and using the special emollient cream prescribed for her face, she whiled away the recovery period reading and watching television.

There seemed to be a lot of road-works going on in the locality, with pneumatic drills constantly tearing the air with their ear-splitting chatter, but she did not allow the noise to bother her. She had better things to do now; a whole new world beckoned.

Mr. Parker was very pleased with the results of the surgery, although to her it looked as if she had been in the boxing ring with Frank Bruno. The surgeon had warned her that at first it would look pretty awful, but that a week would bring about a total transformation. The face staring back at her in the mirror resembled a piece of raw steak from the supermarket, but she knew she must be patient.

She spent the first week resting and following Mr.

Parker's instructions, willing the puffiness and bruising to heal quickly. Adhering to the strict diet, her weight continued to fall, and she established a regime of simple yoga exercises to do every day.

By the seventh day, as promised, she was looking pretty good. No longer afraid to look in the mirror she inspected every inch of the new skin. 'It's amazing what these lasers can do!' she thought.

It was ten days before she felt confident enough to leave her flat to go shopping. She was determined to change her life completely now that the operation had given her a new look, and her shape continued to improve as she stuck rigidly to her diet and exercises. The next stage of the metamorphosis was to buy a totally new wardrobe of clothes. She had enjoyed sorting out all her frumpy outfits and bagging them up for the charity shop.

Her savings had virtually all been spent on the clinic and the surgery, so she chose her new clothes with a lot of careful thought and planning. She arrived home after the shopping trip exhausted but very excited.

This was the beginning of her new life. 'No more good old Chubs,' she told herself.

Finally the day came when she had to go back to the office and start work again. That morning she was up very early, nervous but exhilarated. She took great care to apply the light camouflage cream to her new, soft-skinned face and spent a long time doing her hair and eye makeup. This was the most important day of her life. She must get everything just right.

Stepping back from the mirror she surveyed herself critically. The new dress looked stunning and her once-plump body was now svelte and curvy, her hair thick and shining. In the magnifying mirror over the basin she took a final look at her new face. It was unbelievable. She was pretty, she really was. It had been worth every penny.

She carefully applied her lipstick and took one final look at herself. Even she could not believe the transformation. This beautiful young woman was hardly recognisable as the plain and plump old 'Chubs'. The butterfly had emerged from the chrysalis.

Closing the door behind her, she left the flat with her heart full of hope for the future, and headed for the bus stop with a spring in her step and a smile on her face.

She did not even see the car. The witnesses all told the police the same thing - that she had stepped straight off the kerb into the path of the oncoming vehicle. The driver had not stood a chance. It had seemed to those who had seen the accident that she had been looking the wrong way up the street as she started across.

Perhaps she was new to the area, or had been away for a while. After all, it was only during the last week that the one-way system had been changed to the opposite direction.

As the ambulance pulled away from the scene, the young paramedic looked down at the woman on the stretcher.

'What a bloody shame,' he said, his face full of sadness and pity. 'Such a beautiful girl. Looks like a model. Poor kid - what a waste.'

He shook his head sadly as he gently pulled the snow-white sheet up over her face - such a beautiful face.

HIDE AND SEEK

It was the early days of the Restoration. Charles II was now on the throne of England and the country was once again rejoicing in its Monarchy. The dark days of Cromwell were behind them and the people were looking forward to a settled future under their King.

There was at last a sense of hope throughout the land as the years of discontent and harshness rolled away. A new dawn was breaking, a new era beginning. The people could see a bright horizon, after so many bleak years.

In the beautiful countryside of Hertfordshire the Royalist Fairfax family resided in their magnificent mansion. With dozens of servants at their beck and call, and King Charles now rightfully restored to the throne, life was good. The six children, four boys and two girls, enjoyed the privileges of their rank. James Fairfax had made his fortune as a silk merchant in the City of London and the family had moved out into the country just before poor King Charles I had been beheaded by the Puritans.

The Royalists had lost many good men during the Civil War, and James had thanked God many times that his sons were too young to fight. He himself was no soldier, and had watched the defeat of the King's men with growing dismay and despair. Cromwell's rise to power had heralded in a period of misery and gloom for the country, and the Fairfax family had moved out of London to escape the rigours of the harsh city laws.

The years under Cromwell and his Roundheads had been difficult and fraught with danger, but the family had survived unscathed. Many of their friends had not been so lucky, losing their possessions and some their lives during the harsh repression. Many others had fled overseas to escape from the Puritanical and military regime.

Now Cromwell was dead, and the country was beginning to settle back into a peaceful period. The clouds had lifted and the future looked secure. Charles II presided over a happy and easy-going Court in London, and all over the country the prospects for a better life under the new King grew brighter every day. James Fairfax was determined that his family would grow up surrounded by love and happiness after the dark days of Cromwell. A kindly man, he and his adored wife Abigail made sure that their six children enjoyed the good things in life whilst instilling in them both discipline and good manners.

The children spent their days playing games and riding their ponies on the estate. The older children were taught at home by a variety of tutors, their knowledge of history, geography, Latin and French improving every day in their schoolroom at the top of the big house. Rows of books on every conceivable subject filled the shelves of the huge library, and they read avidly whenever time allowed.

As far as the eye could see, this was Fairfax land. Their heritage. Acres of lush green pastures, woodland and lakes, beautiful rose gardens and a magnificent orchard just to the south of the old house. Beyond the high brick wall lay the vegetable gardens, lovingly tended by the family gardeners.

The eldest son John would inherit the house and grounds one day when James passed on, but for now their lives were filled with fun and laughter. Life was good under the new King, and the Fairfax family was blessed with good health and sufficient wealth to enjoy it to the full.

It was a happy household, the sound of children's voices ringing through the spacious rooms, lending a vibrancy to the lives of all in residence there. In short, the family lived a charmed existence, continually thanking the good Lord for his blessings.

Sarah and John were playing Hide and Seek, racing from room to room in the huge house. There were so many places they could hide themselves. It was a favourite family game, and today the two children had spent many hours taking it in turns to hide and to seek. The two eldest in the family, they were very similar in appearance. Tall and slender with fair hair and blue eyes, they were inseparable companions, always together.

They had been playing for hours, and now John was beginning to tire of the game, but little Mary had decided that she wanted to play too. She was only five, but her brother and sister would allow her just one game before they all had to go to the nursery for their tea. Clapping her chubby little hands with joy, her eyes alight with excitement, she followed her brother out of the hall and up the long curving staircase.

She was a pretty little girl, with long brown curls tumbling to her shoulders and big brown eyes. She had a loving nature and the whole family adored her; she was the youngest, their baby.

John was helping her to find a hiding place while Sarah closed her eyes and counted to one hundred. They ran from room to room to find somewhere suitable, and John stopped in one of the many bedrooms. He pointed to the big oak linen chest at the bottom of the four-poster bed, and opened the heavy lid. It was a bit of a struggle for him, but he managed it.

It was half-empty, the clean white cotton sheets laid neatly at the bottom, but plenty of room for little Mary to hide on top of them. She was a bit wary of climbing inside but her big brother persuaded her that Sarah would not find her here. It was the perfect hiding place, one they had not used before. He would come and collect her when Sarah admitted defeat. She would give up very quickly, John told his baby sister.

The little girl, dressed in a beautiful long red velvet dress with a white lace collar, scrambled over the edge of the chest and lay down on the freshly-laundered linen, curling herself up into a comfortable position. She cuddled her favourite doll, which went everywhere with her, hugging it tightly to her chest as John kissed her quickly and they both giggled to think how poor Sarah would be looking for her in all the old hiding places.

They heard Sarah call out that she was coming, ready or not, and John shut the heavy lid down over his little sister. He found that it would not stay tightly closed with Mary inside, so he pushed down harder until the big brass lock engaged. To make sure it stayed shut he turned the key in the lock, whispering to his sister to keep quiet until either he or Sarah came to fetch her.

'It won't be long,' he said, 'not long at all.'

Mary did not like it inside the chest. It was very dark and silent, but she did not want to spoil the game so she stayed very quiet. She knew it would only be a little while before either Sarah gave up looking for her or John came to let her out, so she made herself as comfortable as she could on top of the sheets.

After a while she became quite sleepy, and being only five years old, found it an easy matter to doze off in the darkness on top of the crisp clean linen. With her thumb in her mouth and her doll clasped tight in her chubby little arms, Mary fell into a deep sleep.

Snug and warm inside the chest, shut away from the outside world, she did not hear John's sudden scream of terror as he tripped over one of the family spaniels at the top of the stairs. She did not hear his heart-stopping cries as he tumbled down the long staircase, turning over and over in his fall. She did not hear the ensuing pandemonium in the house as everyone rushed to the still body of the slim young boy lying spread-eagled on the marble hall floor.

As panic engulfed the household and her brother was carried to the nearest sofa, little Mary slept on in her secret hiding-place. She remained oblivious to the accident, to the tears and the heartache.

Her brother, sadly, would die from head injuries sustained in the fall, but she could not know that. Nor could she know how they had searched for her. Desperation taking hold, they had looked everywhere for the little girl, calling her name all through the big house, search parties scouring the acres of land outside.

As the hours went by and the family's grief intensified, Mary remained hidden and undiscovered. The search for her became more and more frantic as the baby of the family was nowhere to be found. Every man, woman and child working on the estate combed the woods, the fields and the outbuildings while the household servants searched the house from attic to cellars, but there was not a sign of the child.

Sarah had no idea where her little sister was hiding. Sobbing uncontrollably as John was taken to his room by his distraught parents, she led the searchers to all their favourite hiding places, but Mary was not in any of them. The other children joined in the frantic hunt for their baby sister as the enormity of the tragedy that had befallen the family that day became clear to them.

Struggling with their grief at the loss of their brother they searched desperately for Mary, only too aware that John alone had known where she was hiding. They could not ask him - they could never ask him. Their sobs could be heard all over the Fairfax estate as they screamed her name over and over again, but to no avail.

No-one checked inside the linen chest. They could all see that it was locked so she could hardly be in there. In their haste to search the house and grounds the first cursory glance over the big oak chest was enough. The huge brass lock was engaged and the key turned. They moved on to the next room without a second look, calling her name with increasing panic in their voices.

Mary woke after a long sleep and wondered for a while where she was. Then she remembered. She was very stiff and tried to move her little arms and legs, the doll falling sideways as she moved. There was not much room inside the chest, but she wriggled about until she was more comfortable, feeling for her doll in the darkness and tucking it into the crook of her arm.

She was beginning to get scared. It was a long time for a little girl to be shut up in the dark. Mary began to call out for John and Sarah, but nobody came to find her. Hugging her doll more tightly to her, she felt the tears begin to flow. Tired and hungry now, she wanted to get out of the linen chest. She cried and screamed but still the heavy lid stayed tightly shut.

Unable to move very much, and sobbing with fright, the little girl called out as loudly as she could until she grew hoarse from the effort. Finally exhausted, she slept again, as is the way with small children.

She opened her eyes as she heard the sound of the key being turned in the lock. At last someone had found her. She began to cry again, and called out for her mother.

The light streaming into the chest hurt her eyes. The lid was lifted right back until she could see two men looking down at her. Who were they? She did not recognise them. They were strangers. Mary was terrified.

She tried to lift her hand to shield her eyes against the light, but she could not move. As she saw a hand reach down to touch her she opened her mouth to scream . . .

One of the men reached down into the chest and touched the pretty red velvet dress. He drew his hand back sharply as it came in contact with the little girl. The two looked at each other, shock etched clearly on their faces. They had been researching the mystery surrounding the Fairfax family in the mid-1600's, and were systematically working their way through the manor house now owned by the National Trust.

They had been trying to establish what had happened to the youngest child of the family, a little girl only five years old, who had disappeared without trace the same day as her brother had died in a tragic accident in the house. They had not expected to solve the puzzle, simply hoped to find some kind of explanation if at all possible. Many had tried before, but all had failed.

All the furniture stood in its original place, the house looking as it did in Restoration times when Charles II was King of England. The linen chest was a fine piece of carved oak, a collector's item. To judge by the condition of the big brass lock, it had not been opened for a very long time. An oversight on someone's part, but a bonus for them. Whatever was inside would be a part of history; treasure trove perhaps, they had thought.

The lock had proved very difficult to open, but at last their perseverance had been rewarded. With bated breath they had lifted up the heavy oak lid and looked down into the interior of the magnificent linen chest.

Little Mary Fairfax stared up at them, her favourite doll still in her arms.

The two historians stared back in total disbelief at the tiny skeleton in its once-beautiful red velvet dress. Whatever they had anticipated, nothing had prepared them for this. They had found the missing child - the mystery of the Fairfax family was finally solved.

Mary was so pleased that someone had at last come to find her.

She could not know that the game of Hide and Seek had lasted over three hundred years . . .

NUMBER 1

She held onto his hand tightly as they walked down the tunnel towards the Arena. The crowd was chanting the name of the group as the excitement of the evening built up. The venue had sold out as soon as the tickets had gone on sale and the place was packed to capacity.

The supporting act had warmed up the audience, and now the fans awaited the arrival of their idols, stamping their feet and yelling for them to appear.

At 23, and standing 6'2" in his socks, the handsome young drummer was her youngest child, still her little boy. She was so proud of him, of his achievements. Without him, she wouldn't be here tonight. He had become one of the world's best-known rock drummers over the past few months, and tonight she would once again see him with his group take the roof off the hall with their mighty sound.

They were good, very good. In the cut-throat world of rock music, they were the current high fliers, their CDs and albums selling in their millions; gold and platinum discs for each new release. The two guitarists and the keyboard player had joined the young drummer to form this group only six months ago, and their singer Ricky had been poached from a local pub band. They had travelled all over Europe on their first ever tour, headlining concerts in every major city, and now they were on the last leg, home in Wembley Arena.

After a two-week break, they were to fly to the States and begin a major tour as top billing - a fantastic achievement for such a new band. Her pride knew no bounds as she peeked out from behind the curtain, and watched the hundreds of fans stamping, yelling and calling for their idols. She turned to the lads, and gave each one a good luck kiss. They hugged her, all so excited to be here.

Wembley at last, their dream . . . and the American tour coming up. Life was good, very good.

The speed of their success had taken them all by surprise. Only in their wildest dreams could they have hoped for such a meteoric rise to fame. Their first hit had gone straight into the charts at No. 1, followed by appearances on MTV, Top of the Pops and all the usual shows. Worldwide sales of their CDs were phenomenal. Then a chance to go on the road had suddenly occurred when a major blues band had split up and a replacement group was needed urgently.

Their musical talents had been recognised at once, and the concerts were so successful that the agents had fallen over themselves to sign up the group. Only the singer had reservations after years of experience in the industry, warning the lads of the pitfalls and advising caution. It was obvious, however, that for the moment at least, they could do no wrong. This was their time in the sun; everything they touched turned to gold.

It was all happening so fast, and it was simply magic. They were all committed to putting everything into their music, giving the fans value for money, and loving every second of fame. Determined to live for the moment, they were only too well aware that many groups before them had been flavour of the month before descending equally quickly into obscurity.

The group stood behind the curtain just a few moments longer, the adrenalin pumping, drinking in the atmosphere. They were all dressed in black leather jeans and black T-shirts with the group's name on the front and the tour dates on the back. Out in the Arena the noise was deafening. The crowd was ready and eager. So were they.

The drummer kissed his mum again, and she smiled up into his face, sharing this very special moment with her young son. The group members wished each other good luck, and yelling back at their fans, ran onto the stage to the roars of the crowd. They acknowledged the cheers, and picking up their instruments as the drummer sat behind his huge semi-circle of drums and cymbals, began their first number, revelling in the fantastic atmosphere of their home city.

Dry ice billowed smoke out onto the stage, and the flashing multi-coloured laser lighting illuminated the stage as they launched themselves whole-heartedly into their music. Huge amplifiers at the edge of the stage blasted their songs out into the packed Arena.

Their well-rehearsed act raised the roof, the singer's powerful voice belting out the words over the heavy rock music. As the first song finished, the crowd erupted again, and the electricity in the air was tangible. The band continued with tracks from their albums, the audience joining in, until everyone in the Arena was hoarse from singing and shouting.

The fans stood and roared them on, and they gave it everything they had, as they always did. On and on they played, giving a performance to remember. They drank in the atmosphere, loving every second of their music and lifting the crowd to new heights as they played their hearts out.

Ricky, as ever, sang superbly, complementing the musical talents of the others in the group. They knew their craft inside out, and the yelling fans appreciated every note of the concert.

As the evening began to draw to a close, the security men were having trouble holding back the fans as they surged towards the stage, but it was a good-natured crowd, everyone having the time of their life. Flowers rained onto the stage, acknowledging the band's tremendous performance, along with notes, cards and photos from hopeful young ladies in the audience.

As the last number reverberated around the famous hall, with several encores, the crowd sang along with the band, waving cigarette lighters with their flames aglow to sing the concert to a close.

Ricky stood in the spotlight as the music faded away, shaking hands with those lucky enough to be able to reach over the lights. Then, turning with arms raised to the crowd, clapping with them and thanking them for their support, the singer reached for a bottle of mineral water and drank deeply. The fans kept yelling for more, but it was time for the band to finish for the evening - they had already played long past their original projected time.

Turning away from the microphone with a final wave to the crowds, and facing the band, the tired but elated singer walked back to the young drummer, picking up some of the bunches of flowers thrown by the fans. Hugging the others as they joined in the general mayhem on and off stage, exhausted from their efforts but thrilled at the success of the evening, Ricky reached a hand up to the drummer as he wiped the sweat from his face with a towel.

Sweating from his exertions and out of breath, his eyes shining with delight, he reached over his drum-kit to give Ricky a huge bear-hug.

They grinned at each other, and he yelled at her over the noise, 'I'm so proud of you, Mum. Beats the hell out of singing in the pubs, doesn't it?'

GHOSTS

They hammered on the door of the old house, calling out to whoever was inside that they needed help. Their car had hit a tree at the bottom of the driveway and they had both been knocked unconscious; for how long neither knew. Their injuries seemed slight, a few cuts and bumps, but they were in shock and needed to use a telephone to summon help. It was pitch dark now and this was the only house they could find.

No-one answered their frantic knocking. Susan tried the big wrought iron handle and the door creaked inwards. Her husband, holding her round the waist to support her as they both staggered into the hall of the big house, stood looking around. His head was hurting and he could feel the trickle of blood running down his face. Susan was on the verge of fainting and he held her up as he called out for someone to come and help them.

His voice echoed around the hallway. It was very dark inside the house, the only light coming from a few candles he could see on the mantelpiece over the stone fireplace.

'This is very creepy,' he thought to himself. There did not seem to be anyone at home. He led Susan over to the nearest chair and gently sat her down. Her skin was incredibly hot, he noticed; she must have a fever. She looked extremely pale and he was very concerned that she may have internal injuries from the crash. Apart from a bruise on her forehead he could see no outward signs of any damage, but they had to be sure.

He called out again, louder this time, but there was still no response. They seemed to be alone in this old place, and it was unnerving on top of the shock of the crash.

They had lost their way on the road to Exeter and he had no idea where they were now. The car was a write-off and they needed help urgently. Where the hell was everyone?

He left Susan in the chair while he looked into the downstairs rooms, calling out all the time. 'It's really weird,' he thought. 'Like stepping back in time.' The whole place seemed to be furnished in a very old-fashioned style and the marble hall floor and the wood-panelled walls were from a bygone era.

Michael could find no light switches nor could he see any sign of a telephone anywhere. It was so dark he took up one of the candles in its holder to light his way. He looked back to check that Susan was still conscious, and in the flickering candlelight he saw a movement on the wide staircase.

He lifted the candle up higher and found himself looking at a young girl, her face white and terrified as she stared back at him. She opened her mouth and screamed loudly, making him jump. Susan cried out in fright and he involuntarily dropped the candle.

Moving quickly over to his wife in the darkness he held her tightly. She was shaking with fear. They clung together and he noticed again how hot she felt. Susan's eyes were wide with terror. 'Who was she?' she asked him, her voice shrill with fear. 'Did . . . did you see what she was wearing?'

Michael nodded. In the few seconds he had caught sight of the girl in the candle's flickering light he had noticed that she was dressed in the sort of clothes he had seen in pictures of the Elizabethan age, hundreds of years before. It was all very weird; the eerie old house, the strangely-dressed girl.

Where were they, for God's sake?

'Michael, I'm so tired, so hot. You must find help, I

need a doctor. Please Michael! This is such an awful place, so dark and old. It may even be haunted. Oh God! She could be a ghost! Oh Michael, please - help me.' Susan was sobbing now, tears running down her face.

He looked down at his young wife in despair. Grabbing another candle in its holder he began shouting as he ran up the stairs to find the girl again. There must be more people here, it was a huge house.

At the end of the corridor on the landing he could just make out a small group of men and women. They were huddled together staring at him in fright. He tried to calm himself and talk rationally to them as he approached, but he was desperate to get help for Susan. He saw that they were all dressed in the same style of clothes as the girl he had seen on the staircase. Vaguely he wondered if this could be a fancy dress party, but there was no music, no noise at all in the big house.

The candle flickered as he walked quickly towards the people at the end of the landing, wondering why they seemed so afraid of him. They appeared to be mesmerised by his presence, standing immobile as he drew closer to them.

As he approached the little group the women screamed and hid behind the men. They too held candles, and Michael realised that he probably looked an awful sight in this light - enough to make anyone scream. His head was bloody, he knew, and his clothes in tatters where he had dragged himself then Susan out of the wrecked car. 'No wonder they're frightened,' he thought. Seeing him like this, it was quite understandable.

He continued to talk quietly to them explaining his dilemma, feeling himself getting very hot as he drew near them. They were staring at him in sheer terror now, eyes wide and mouths working as if preparing to cry out again. He came up to the first man and tried to speak to him. He recoiled immediately and as Michael reached out to touch his shoulder, his hand went straight through the other's body as if it wasn't there.

He stood gaping in disbelief as the man backed further away, everyone in the small group staring at Michael with abject fear in their eyes, obviously petrified by his appearance. He reached out again to touch the man but once more his hand sliced through the air. Through . . . *nothing!*

Michael started to tremble, the candle shaking in his hand. His mind was racing. The people, the clothes, the old house. 'Oh God,' he thought, 'they ARE ghosts, bloody ghosts! Susan was right!' His horror mounting, he turned quickly and ran back down the corridor to the staircase.

He raced down the stairs as Susan turned her head towards him. 'What's happening?' she cried out in panic as she saw the fear in his face. Without a word Michael pulled her up out of the chair towards the front door. He was once again aware of how hot she was, but he was in no mood to stop here now. He himself felt as if he had a fever; he was sweating profusely, but that was the least of his worries at the moment.

Michael half-carried his wife through the big wooden front door out into the black night. It was cold now but they had to get away from this haunted place - this nightmare from Hell. They would go and sit by the wreckage of the car until it was light enough to find a phone box. Not an ideal solution, but the only haven for the moment.

At least they would be away from this . . . this, God what was it? An apparition? Their minds playing tricks after they had hit their heads in the crash? Whatever it was, they were getting out of here as soon as possible. The thought of those ghostly people made him shudder.

He had to pick Susan up as she was now too weak to walk. Staggering under her weight he realised that she was burning up with fever. She was unbelievably hot; he must get help soon, very soon or she would slip into unconsciousness and may not recover.

Hell, what a dreadful place this was. Susan was moaning quietly in his arms as he tried to reach the wrecked car as quickly as possible. They had to get away from the house, away from those people.

He concentrated on carrying his wife as gently as he could, and was relieved to find himself finally at the end of the driveway. The old building was behind them now, lost in the darkness.

Turning in the direction of the crashed car he almost dropped Susan as his eyes took in the scene before him.

The car was still embedded in the tree. There was not much of it left now. It was entirely burnt out. A shell. He stood in shock and horror at the sight of the two bodies in the front seats. Susan was staring too, her mouth open, stark terror etched on her face. He was aware again of the searing heat in their bodies as they stood staring at the remains of their car.

The awful realisation dawned on them both at the same time. They had not survived the car crash after all. They were still in their seats inside the burned-out wreck.

No wonder the people in the house had been so scared. Susan and Michael stared open-mouthed at each other in fear and dread as the terrible truth of the situation hammered home.

It was not the Elizabethans who were lost in time. It was them. THEY were the intruders.

THEY were the ghosts!

ANGEL

She was stunning, simply stunning. He watched her walk into the bar and he caught his breath. Short blonde hair framing a heart-shaped face and the biggest blue eyes he had ever seen. Her silver dress clung to her body in all the right places - and, 'my God,' he thought to himself, 'does she have all the right places!'

Ignoring the open-mouthed stares of the men standing or just lolling about in the small taverna, she walked over to the barman and ordered a Buck's Fizz. 'Expensive tastes too,' he thought. A champagne lady in all respects. He could not take his eyes off her, and neither could anyone else in the bar. Here on the remote northern coast of the tiny Greek island of Kefalonia he had not expected to meet anyone interesting, let alone such a gorgeous creature.

Nobody here was aware of the reason for him being on the island. He was in hiding; in fear of his life. As a minor minion working for the Mob in New York his greed had finally proved uncontrollable, handling as he did so much of their money. He had tried for a long time just to do his job, and he had done it well until that fateful day. He had been a rising star, one of the Don's favourites. But he had been sorely tempted by the sheer amount of cash flowing through his hands.

The Don was always generous to his ground troops, and it had been a good time for them all. He would never know what had made him take that last huge payment; it was a spur-of-the-moment decision. As he drove to the rendezvous with the briefcase on the seat beside him, he had found himself heading instead for the airport.

He took the first flight across to San Francisco and set about establishing a new identity as fast as he could, before his Mafia bosses realised what had happened. There was no doubt in his mind as to what would happen to him if they caught up with him.

He knew that as soon as he did not turn up at the rendezvous they would begin the search for him. At first they would not be suspicious - he was trusted implicitly by his comrades, a trust built up over the years. They would assume that he had met with an accident, or been waylaid somewhere. Only after his disappearance could be neither explained nor excused would they embark on a full-scale search. It was a great deal of money - their money - and nobody crossed these men and lived to tell the tale.

He did not have much time. He had used the Mob's underground contacts on the West Coast to provide him with a false passport and papers, spinning them a story about a job he had to do incognito for his boss. He had changed his normal fair hair colour to jet black with a temporary dye, and added a pair of thick-rimmed glasses. The transformation was immediate; he looked totally different.

The men working on his papers would themselves soon be traced, this he knew, the trail leading his pursuers to them, so it was imperative that he leave the country at once. The two million dollars inside the briefcase would set him up in a hideaway where they would never find him. The die was cast; no turning back now.

He had to put as many miles between himself and his hunters as fast as possible.

He consulted the airline schedules in the taxi on the way to the airport. Where could he run to? Where could he hide? Vaguely he remembered snatches of conversations he had had as a youngster with an elderly Greek lady who lived near his family in New York. She had talked endlessly about her home country and about the many small islands; how beautiful and tranquil they were. Few tourists except in the cities.

At the airport he had bought a first-class ticket to Athens, his new passport accepted without question. The Don's boys were superb at their craft - nothing was beyond their capabilities. He had grinned wryly as he walked through the departure gate. He was a lawyer from Oklahoma now, it would seem from the documentation. 'A suitably unlikely change of persona,' he thought to himself with a smirk.

His nerves were beginning to bother him as he sat in the first-class lounge, but as soon as the plane left the ground he settled back in his seat with a glass of whisky and began to plan his future. He was feeling a little safer up there above the clouds. He would not allow himself even to think about what was happening back on the ground in New York. He must not lose his grip on the situation, or he would be a dead man.

From the tourist guide at Athens airport he discovered that there were indeed a number of small islands to choose from. He liked his comforts, had no intention of roughing it, and after taking a couple of hours to read through the information in the tourist guidebooks over a couple more whiskies, he settled on the tiny island of Kefalonia. It did have a tourist season, but at the moment the island was in its winter phase, still warm and very peaceful.

It sounded perfect for his needs, a place to start at least. The airline check-in desk showed a flight leaving for the island later that night, so he booked a ticket and settled down to wait for the next phase of his new life.

He had been here three months now. With the stolen money he had been able to rent a pretty and spacious bungalow on the north coast, very remote but close enough to a small town for him to venture out occasionally. It was lonely here, the rugged scenery a fitting backdrop for a man on the run. The islanders were friendly but not intrusive. It was the perfect spot to think, to plan.

Despite the continual fear that someone would find him, and the knowledge that there would now be a contract out on his life, he began to feel a little more secure with every passing day. Although he was lonely he knew that this was simply a stepping-stone to the next part of his journey.

He planned everything in minute detail, alone in his bungalow with no-one to disturb him. Hour after hour he pored over his paperwork, revising and honing every detail until he was satisfied that there was no flaw, no possibility of mistakes. His very life depended on that.

He planned to make his way to Australia in a few weeks' time. Out there he knew he would find the requisite plastic surgeon to alter his appearance, so necessary to maintain his safety. Once that was done, he could settle anywhere on that huge continent. No-one would ever find him there - a brand new identity and a new face would ensure that.

But tonight, a totally unexpected blonde bombshell had entered his life. Here in this remote corner of the Greek island, in his local taverna - a beautiful woman drinking champagne. Luckily they kept the odd bottle in the cellar, or she'd have been on the Retsina, he mused. Like paint-stripper, that stuff!

She looked around the small bar and caught his eye. Sitting up on the barstool, her slim legs demurely crossed, she was fully aware of the devastating effect she was having upon the local population. The Greeks were staring at this angelic creature with open mouths. 'She's revelling in it,' he thought to himself, and grinned. Never seen anything like it, no doubt. Mind you, neither had he. She was absolutely exquisite in every way. Face, figure, legs - like a model.

She took a cigarette out of her handbag and put it to her lips. He moved like lightning, his gold-plated lighter flickering into life as she bent her head towards it. She smiled her thanks at him and his heart jumped as the big blue eyes looked into his. He then began to talk to her, nervously at first, but she responded without hesitation and soon they were chatting like old friends.

He was aware of the envious stares of the other men, and grinned round at them all as he sat at the bar with the beautiful woman. She was indeed a model, she told him, from Denmark. At the moment she was taking a break from a photographic assignment in Athens, a magazine spread for a swimwear company. She was only here for a couple of days, to find some peace and quiet before returning to the city and more studio work.

They left the bar together in the early hours of the morning, to the despair of the local men left in disarray in the taverna, and walked down the steep path to the beach below the cliff. It was cold and she shivered in the damp night air. The waves were gently lapping the shoreline, and there was a sea mist hanging like an opaque curtain in the air. He suggested that they return to his bungalow for a nightcap; brandy, coffee, whatever she wanted. She grinned at him, and he blushed slightly, returning the grin, knowing that she had read his mind.

Protesting only mildly, she said she should go back to her hotel, really. It was only a taxi ride away in the nearest town. He insisted that she visit the bungalow before she left, secure in the knowledge that at this time of the morning it would be utterly impossible to find a taxi. She obviously did not understand Greek island life. He would suggest when the time came that she stay the night in his guest room. The mere thought of this stunning creature under his roof excited him beyond belief.

He made them both coffee with a dash of brandy to warm them up, and they settled comfortably together on the sofa. He had lit a blazing log fire in the hearth, and they cuddled up close in its cosy glow. The combination of their evening's drinking and the warmth of the room began to work on their senses.

As they sat close together he moved towards her and kissed her gently. She responded immediately; there was no doubt in their minds where this chance meeting would end.

As he turned to look at her beautiful face on the pillow next to his, he had difficulty in believing what had happened that night. Not only was she magnificent to look at, she was the best lover he had ever had. In the dawn light streaming in through the bedroom curtains she looked more than ever like an angel. He lay back, his mind in turmoil.

He had been so lonely during his months on the island. She had been like a breath of fresh air in his life; a few hours with her had turned his solitary existence on its head. He desperately wanted her to stay with him, wherever he ended up on his travels. She had come into his life so unexpectedly and he wanted her to be with him, to share his new life.

She would not need to know about his past. He would cover his tracks so thoroughly they would never find him. God but he wanted this - he had never thought about it before, but now she had changed everything. Just these few hours together had thrown everything into confusion. He must have her with him. He tried to think lucidly but it was impossible.

Lying next to him, sleeping like a baby, she was what he wanted above all else as he started on his new future. He must think this through carefully, he knew his life depended upon it. He could include her in all his plans; the money would cover everything. He must persuade her to come to Australia, to live with him; just be with him.

It was a kind of madness, he realised. He had only just met her, but he could not bear to lose her now. She had to stay with him, or he would go mad.

He bent over to kiss her gently on the lips, and she smiled in her sleep. She may have the looks of an angel, he thought, but she was a devil in bed! Best of both worlds - stunning to look at and a hell of a lover. Tenderly he stroked her soft hair, and watched her wake languidly from her sleep.

The long lashes parted slowly, fluttering for a moment like a butterfly's wings as her deep blue eyes, still sleepy, began to focus on his face. He was utterly entranced; she was so beautiful. He felt his heart pounding as he bent towards her, kissing her again as she stretched luxuriously like a kitten waking from a deep sleep.

Slowly she raised herself up on her elbow and he gazed into those beautiful blue eyes. He could not get his thoughts together. He was mesmerised by her, but he knew he had to work out what to say to her, and persuade her to stay with him. It was all that mattered now.

She smiled so sweetly, so lovingly at him as she lifted her hand towards his face, then gently brushed his forehead with the barrel of the gun. His eyes widened in terror and dreadful understanding in the second before she pulled the trigger.

As the helicopter lifted off from the small island airport the pilot cast a glance over his shoulder at the sole passenger. How could someone so beautiful be such a cold-blooded killer? He shrugged - not his problem. He was simply following orders, providing her means of escape. They paid him well for his flying skills, they always did, and it was not his place to question their orders.

The blonde beauty sat back in her seat as they skimmed over the Ionian Sea. The briefcase containing the stolen money was tucked neatly beneath her feet. Another contract successfully concluded. Her boss in New York would be pleased, she knew.

It had taken them a while to locate him on the island, but they had known she was the one for the job.

It was to be expected - after all, she was the Mafia's top executioner. She laughed as she thought back over the years. They always fell for it, these stupid men. They only wanted her for sex, but it gave her just the opportunity she needed, every time.

How she loved to see the terror in their eyes in those final seconds. She loved the money too, of course, but to see that look on their faces was her real reward. That stunned look of realisation, of horror, of disbelief - it gave her such a high, every time. Better than any drug, and no side effects, just pure ecstasy.

The cold-hearted killer called Angel smiled contentedly to herself as the helicopter droned its way towards Athens.

LOVERS

They strolled along the white sandy beach hand in hand, totally absorbed in each other. It was their wedding anniversary, and they had promised themselves they would have the best holiday of their lives.

After months of planning and saving here they were. They had decided on the Caribbean, and Antigua had looked so lovely in the brochures. It had lived up to all their hopes and dreams. Paradise. The sea was a beautiful blue under the hot summer sun, and this part of the island was well away from the normal tourist areas. Their friendly travel agent had recommended the hotel - quiet and elegant.

They had enjoyed a light lunch of fruit and salad by the hotel pool, and after their stroll along the beach they would return to the hotel for an afternoon sleep while the sun was at its hottest.

They walked slowly, stopping every now and again to share a loving kiss. The couple had met when they were at school and had married as soon as they could on her 18th birthday. He was only 19, and they had met with fierce resistance from both families, but nothing was going to stop them. Each knew they had found their life's partner. The attraction had been immediate; they had become inseparable.

The wedding had been a joyous occasion. Even their parents had had to agree that this was a love-match. The way they looked at each other, their faces glowing with love. Any doubts were dispelled on that day; here was a couple destined to stay together.

A match made in Heaven, if ever there was one.

They shook the sand from their feet as they walked up the steps into the marble hotel lobby. It was indeed an elegant hotel, built in the 1920's, spacious and beautifully decorated. Like everything else about their Caribbean paradise, it was perfect.

Their room was large and cool, the fan on the ceiling lazily moving the air around. Taking off their light clothes they lay together on the king-size bed. Cuddling up close they drifted off to sleep, totally happy and content. Arms wrapped around each other, they dozed the hours away until the sound of the dinner gong woke them and they quickly showered and changed for dinner.

She looked quite beautiful in her pale blue satin dress, the three-string necklace of pearls and matching earrings showing off her light tan to perfection. In her hair she wore a pretty mother-of-pearl slide, bought that morning at the local town market.

As always, he cut a dashing figure in his evening suit, a pure white silk shirt under the black well-cut jacket enhancing his suntanned face. They smiled adoringly at each other - such a handsome couple, and so very much in love. Arm in arm they ambled along the corridor and made their way down the wide staircase to the dining room, admiring again the glittering crystal chandeliers lighting their way.

The food, as always, was magnificent. They enjoyed a wonderful meal and, as a special surprise for them, the band played The Anniversary Waltz. Shyly they took to the floor and, to the cheers of the other hotel guests, danced their way around the room looking for all the world like a couple on their honeymoon.

The Head Waiter brought them a bottle of Dom Perignon champagne in a silver ice bucket, with the compliments of the hotel, and they toasted each other in the candlelight. A huge bouquet of mixed flowers arrived at the table, and he coyly admitted that he had ordered them to be delivered for her. She kissed him tenderly and thanked him for his thoughtfulness on this, their special day.

It was all so romantic. They gazed into each other's eyes and held hands across the table. Lingering there until the room was empty, they took their leave of the smiling staff and made their way out onto the beach.

Their deep love and affection for each other was obvious to the world. He held his beloved wife around her waist as they walked slowly towards the warm ocean, the sand still warm and silky beneath their feet. The sky was clear and brilliantly lit by hundreds of stars. A crescent moon shimmered and glowed in the incandescent starlight. They stood looking in wonder at the spectacle. Never had they seen so many stars. It was another magic moment for them on this perfect night.

It was almost midnight, the last few minutes of their anniversary. He pulled her to him at the edge of the water. She slipped off her shoes and paddled in the warm sea. He did the same.

Glancing at his watch, he whispered softly in her ear. Pulling her head away quickly, she stared up at him in amazement.

'Skinny-dipping!' she exclaimed. *'Skinny-dipping?'*

'Why not?' he grinned mischievously back at her.

'We've never done it before. We should do something really special while it's still our anniversary.'

She giggled. He was right, they should. Looking around nervously, she made the decision. They were totally alone; it was a splendid, warm night and the sea was beautiful, like warm blue velvet.

A little self-conscious at first, they began to take off their clothes and lay them carefully in a heap. As they stood there naked in the starlight he took her in his arms. They kissed gently and lovingly. How lucky they were to share this much love. It was overwhelming at times.

He took her hand and led her into the sea. It was like stepping into a warm bath. They moved slowly into the water until it was up to their shoulders. Still hand-in-hand they began to swim together, revelling in the warmth and the sensuality of the water on their naked bodies.

It was absolute bliss. They swam, they kissed, they caressed each other. Here in the stillness of the Caribbean night, only the sound of the crickets to disturb the tranquillity, they reaffirmed their love for each other. This had been the most wonderful wedding anniversary, one they would treasure forever.

They left the water reluctantly, but it was time to return to the hotel and to their big soft bed. He was becoming increasingly saucy, she thought, and giggled at the thought of the delicious night that lay ahead when they got back to their room.

They stood naked on the sand, drying themselves off with their clothes. She began to giggle again. 'What a spectacle,' she thought, 'but such a delight.' They held each other at the water's edge, not wanting this night to end.

As they dressed and began the short walk back to the hotel, they put their arms around each other, hugging tightly. Heads together, they wandered slowly back towards the brightly-lit building, barefoot and ecstatically happy, carrying their shoes and delighting in the soft sand as it trickled through their toes.

It had been a magical anniversary, wonderful in every way. Blissful perfection.

At the foot of the steps they stopped once more. He bent his head and kissed his adored wife gently on the lips. She returned his kiss with all the love in her heart and smiled up into his face.

'I love you, my sweetheart,' she said softly.

'And I love you too, my darling,' he replied with a cheeky grin.

'BUT,' she continued, 'if you ever tell anyone that I went skinny-dipping tonight, I will not be responsible for my actions!'

He laughed with delight, and hugged her tighter. After all, he reasoned to himself, it wasn't every day you celebrated your 65th wedding anniversary. And just because they were now in their 80's didn't mean they shouldn't strip off and go swimming if the chance presented itself!

'Happy Anniversary, you daft bat,' he whispered as he held her to him, tears of love welling up in his old eyes.

PREMONITION

She should have been content and happy. Her children played around her in the beautiful garden, chasing each other and laughing without a care in the world. Such a lovely bunch of kids, she was so lucky. It was a family to be proud of, without a doubt.

Yet she shivered in the summer sunshine. Deep inside the fear was beginning to rise again. A feeling, nothing more; just a feeling, she told herself. All mothers worried about their children. But she was more than worried. For a long time she had carried this secret with her, not saying a word to anyone. It seemed to her like a cold wind blowing through their lives, a deep intuition that only a mother could feel.

Becoming angry at her inability to fend off these deep-rooted worries, she told herself not to be so silly. Her sons and daughters were all gathered here today for one of their all-too-infrequent family picnics, together for once to celebrate her youngest boy's birthday. It was so very special to see them enjoying themselves with their siblings and she would spoil the day if she continued with this silliness.

She laughed away their repeated requests to join in the rough and tumble, preferring to sit in her chair drinking iced tea and playing with the family dogs. Her husband was out of town until the evening so she had them all to herself until he returned.

Watching the antics of the youngsters, and the way in which they were all having such fun together, her heart overflowed with love at the happy scene. Her dogs by her side and her family around her, she chided herself for these seemingly irrational fears that she could not control.

Relaxed in her chair, her mind drifting lazily in the heat, she sat smiling contentedly at the activities of the children. As she lifted the glass of cool tea to her lips, she was suddenly aware that four of the older ones had stopped hurtling about and were talking animatedly together, sprawling lazily under the magnificent magnolia tree in the corner of the large garden.

Watching them with a mother's pride as they chatted in the shade of the big old tree, she felt once again a cold fear grip her heart. She caught her breath and tried to calm herself. There *was* something wrong, she knew it; instinctively and intuitively, she knew it.

The three brothers and their sister continued chatting and laughing together while their mother struggled desperately to bring her feelings under control. Setting down the glass of iced tea as her hands began to tremble, she twisted her cotton handkerchief around her fingers as the powerful wave of panic swept through her.

What *was* the matter with her? The children were fine, absolutely fine. It was a large family and they were all strong and healthy apart from her one darling daughter who needed constant nursing care. All the others were perfect; good-looking and talented. She had to stop these attacks. Perhaps a visit to the doctor would help.

She could not tell her husband of these irrational fears. He would simply dismiss her as stupid and would tell her so in no uncertain terms. He was not a man to pander to such female feelings; he was far too arrogant to acknowledge a woman's intuition.

To him, a woman's place was in the kitchen and bedroom; he adhered to that male creed with a vengeance.

Turning once again to the quartet under the tree she made herself return their happy smiles and waves.

Overwhelmed by the continuing feeling of unease, she stood up and walked slowly towards them, her legs like jelly. She had to touch them - just to be sure. It was so very, very stupid, she told herself crossly, but she simply could not help it.

She was angry at her total inability to stifle the panic, but the feeling persisted, like a twisted knot in her stomach. How could she worry herself like this? They were such lovely children; she must try harder not to allow her nerves to take control. Maybe the doctor could prescribe a mild tranquilliser. She would make an appointment to see him as soon as possible.

Walking as casually as she could over to the lovely old tree, she sat down on the immaculate lawn with her sons and daughter. They sat close together talking happily for a long time while the rest of the family wore themselves out with their games.

As the evening approached and their father was due home, her son Jack began to take control of the conversation as he so often did. Everyone listened when he talked; he had so much to say about so many things. They loved to hear his eloquent and knowledgeable stories about life in general.

Gradually the younger family members joined the group, and they all sat beneath the tree, eyes fixed on the good-looking young man, totally under his charismatic spell. The charm of his Irish ancestors flowed through his ceaseless chatter.

His mother watched with pride as her son held the gathering captivated by his spellbinding rhetoric. Hugging two of the little ones to her as one of the dogs licked her face, she listened and laughed with them all, at ease now with her children. The panic had lessened, the knot in her stomach unwound.

He took after his father, she thought - two peas in a pod.

As Jack finished telling the last story there was a gale of laughter from the assembled company. He was so funny, so clever and so very handsome. She felt herself bursting with pride at his accomplishments. And he wasn't the only one - all her sons were destined to have great careers, of that she had no doubt.

Soon it was time to go indoors and get ready for dinner. As they stood up and brushed their clothes down, her pretty daughter kissed Jack lightly on the cheek as their mother watched with a heart full of love. The younger children scampered on ahead as her four beautiful young people hugged their mother and they all began to follow the youngsters towards the house.

Without warning it happened again. From out of nowhere she felt the tingle in her spine as icy fingers of fear crept once more around her heart. She looked in despair at her daughter and the three boys, young adults on the threshold of life.

What *was* this that she felt? She loved them all so much - too much, perhaps. Was that why she was so scared for their futures? She could not rationalise this fear, this premonition of impending loss. It weighed so heavily on her.

They were her babies, her future. Nothing must happen to break the spell, nothing!

Jack smacked his sister lightly on the behind and shouted; 'Race you all inside!' Running ahead like a naughty little boy, his face was alight with that magic smile of his. His mother could not help but smile too.

'You're a little devil, my lad,' she called after him as the others began to chase him.

'You just watch yourself, John Fitzgerald Kennedy - they'll catch up with you one day.'

ONE MINUTE IN TIME

They stood facing each other across No Man's Land,
two young soldiers from different countries. One
English, one German. The war had been dragging on for
years now with so very many deaths on both sides.
Thousands upon thousands of young men from all the
countries involved in the dreadful conflict had died or
been wounded, and still the guns roared.

The King's army set against the Kaiser's army, on the
fields of France and Belgium. A whole generation of
men had been lost here on foreign soil, at sea and in the
air. Soldiers, sailors and airmen - fathers, brothers, sons.
All loved by someone, but now gone forever. The world
would never be the same again; a way of life had ceased
to exist, wiped out by man's inhumanity to man.

Here in the mud of France they stood glaring their
hatred across the intervening strip of land, neutral
territory. Their units had pulled back that morning,
leaving the two soldiers behind. The Tommies and their
German enemies had left the battleground to bury their
dead and tend their wounded. The two young men were
the last soldiers to leave. Each had orders to burn any
classified papers left in their camps after the hasty
retreat so that they could not fall into enemy hands.

Their tasks completed, they had been about to leave
this hellhole when they had spotted each other on this
cold and fateful morning. With the rumour that an
armistice was imminent, neither had any wish to remain
here a second longer than necessary, but they were,
above all else, soldiers.

Trained in deadly warfare, neither man would leave his

post whilst an enemy remained dangerously poised such a short distance away.

The sky above was leaden, the swollen black clouds threatening yet another deluge of rain to swamp the acres of filthy mud, the last resting place of many a young man. It was so cold, so bleak. Caked in mud and wretchedly miserable, both men stood their ground, neither prepared to be the first to back away.

The English lad held his rifle at the ready, waiting for the German to take just one step across the barbed wire barrier. The German soldier watched him like a hawk. Still as statues they waited, each ready to fire his gun should the other make a move towards the wire. For almost twenty minutes now they had remained motionless, frozen in time as they kept their close watch on each other, suspicious and wary and utterly exhausted.

Unwilling to be the first to fire, each man waited for his opposite number to lose his nerve and take that final, fatal step.

As it gradually became apparent to each that neither was about to move forward to the barrier, the English soldier very slowly lowered his rifle from the firing position. The German, staring down the barrel of his own weapon, saw and carefully mirrored the action, at the same time taking a packet of cigarettes out of his tunic pocket. He lit one and drew deeply on it, never taking his eyes off the man standing opposite him.

The swarthy young Yorkshireman grinned to himself, relieved at the break in tension, and took his own cigarettes out to light one. The two young men, still very wary of each other, now stood savouring their cigarettes as the smoke from the previous days' battles drifted around them.

It was like a scene from Hell. The acres of filthy mud around the trenches were littered with burned-out field artillery, bodies of men and horses lying where they had fallen. Cloaked in a heavy grey pall of smoke and mist, the stench of the battleground was overpowering but they had grown used to it during the long terrifying weeks. Now that both armies had withdrawn from that sector there was an eerie stillness about the place.

They could still hear the guns in the distance, but here in this deserted part of Northern France, where so many brave young men had met their deaths, it seemed that they were detached from the war; the Great War as it would be known for all time. The 'war to end all wars,' they said; but history would prove them wrong.

The fair-haired soldier from Frankfurt had been in the German army for only two years and had been fighting in France for the whole of that time. Like his English counterpart across the wire, he had lost many good friends in this alien country. All he wanted was for the war to end so that he could go home and start his life again. A normal life; not this madness.

In his wallet he carried photographs of his family back in Germany, and the pretty girl he would marry as soon as he got home. He had said many prayers that he would join her before too long, and this was to be his last day in France, his journey back to Frankfurt already planned meticulously in his mind.

Watching from his side of the divide the Englishman, 'Tommy', as the British soldiers were called by the Germans, saw the blond figure finish his cigarette and throw away the butt. He did likewise and decided to move right up to the barbed wire, as close as he could without actually stepping onto the neutral ground. He watched with a wry grin as the German did the same on his side of the barrier, and they both stood once again facing each other across No Man's Land, up to their knees in mud.

One Christmas Day - it seemed so long ago now - the

two armies had called a truce and played a game of football together on a muddy strip of land exactly like the one across which the two soldiers faced each other now. Christmas carols had echoed through the air that day, sung loudly in German and English, but it had been only a short-lived break in hostilities. The guns had started up again almost before the last notes of 'Silent Night' had been carried away on the winter wind.

'Fritz', the common name used by the British army for their enemy counterparts, smiled across at his sole companion on this hellish plain and gave him a cheeky wave. The stocky Yorkshireman, acknowledging the insanity of the situation, returned both smile and wave. He too had prayed many times for an end to the fighting. Each rival nation believed they had God on their side in this 'war of wars', never questioning the final outcome of the seemingly unending nightmare.

He picked up his rifle slowly, pointing it into the air to show that he had no intention now of firing at the blond soldier across the mud from him. The gesture was copied by the German and both young men stood at ease, their rifles on their shoulders. Two men alone in a crazy world.

Surrounded by the dead, life seemed very precious at that moment.

As they began to relax in mutual acceptance of the absurdity of their situation and the hope that they would leave the battlefield unscathed, fate intervened yet again in their lives. There was a sudden explosion away to the left of their position, a distant weapon of destruction unleashing its deadly fire. Both men jumped, startled by the unexpected intrusion upon their thoughts.

The young German, unnerved by the noise, brought his rifle back into the firing position. The English soldier, seeing the sudden movement across the wire, did the same and aimed his heavy rifle towards him. Neither man moved - they were enemies again, the short-lived respite over.

They stood once more as opposing forces. Two young men, weary of battle and the horrors of warfare. Their rifles levelled at each other, the soldiers waited, sweating with fear and dread. The minutes ticked by. They watched each other along the barrels of their rifles, nerves in shreds and fingers tight on the triggers.

There was silence now all around them. They seemed to be lost in time and space. Just the two of them. Alone.

There were no more guns firing, no repetition of the echo they had heard. Slowly the men began to lower their rifles again, fully alert but desperate to regain the ground they had lost. As they struggled to compose themselves and revert to their earlier lighter mood the sky grew even darker above them. They watched the clouds gather over their heads as the rain began to lash down in torrents, and the lightning streaked across the sky. Looking across at each other they exchanged grins, each shrugging his shoulders in a gesture of mock despair as they quickly became drenched by the downpour.

When it came, the sudden massive thunderclap was deafening. So unexpected and so near, it sounded for all the world as if they were being fired on from close quarters. Their reactions were immediate and instinctive.

There was a double report, echoing across the deserted fields and reverberating off into the distance. There was no-one alive in that God-forsaken corner of the world to see what had happened, the terrible ending to the young men's last day on duty.

Both soldiers had fired at the same time, their bullets striking home.

The man from Frankfurt lay dead from a wound to the head; his English adversary was alive but barely so. He had been hit just below the heart and with no medical help available, he too would die very shortly. The young soldiers had mistaken the thunder for gunfire, and with their nerves already in tatters, had responded accordingly.

Above their bodies in the dark, sombre sky the big black crows began to circle. The muddy fields had already provided rich pickings for the malevolent birds; now they had yet more fresh bones to pick clean.

As silence fell once more over the battlefield the two young men lay in the mud, their horrific deaths added to the countless thousands already listed on both sides. The rain poured relentlessly down on them, forming great lakes over the acres of muddy war zone and filling the deserted trenches which had been home to so many men over the months. It seemed as though the heavens were trying to wash away all traces of the carnage and bloodshed, to obliterate the scenes of horror and cleanse the land of its battle scars.

On his outstretched wrist the Yorkshire lad wore the new watch his young bride had given him for his birthday on his last leave in England. They had been married for only a short time before he had returned to France, and the watch had been his pride and joy.

The glass was smashed now, and the watch had stopped as he fell to the ground with the fatal bullet in his chest.

As the final supreme irony of the war for both the young soldiers, the hands of the watch would chronicle for ever the time of their deaths that cold winter morning in the flooded fields of Northern France at 11.01.

One minute into history. One minute in time. One minute past the 11th hour of the 11th day of the 11th month in the year of our Lord Nineteen Hundred and Eighteen.

LACK OF THOUGHT

He sat at his desk with his head in his hands. The words just would not come. He had not a single idea in his head, and the deadline was fast approaching.

Writer's block, they called it. It was driving him mad, sitting here surrounded by bits of paper lying all over the floor where he had thrown them in temper and frustration. He had to get out for a while, take a walk in the fresh air. It had been dawn when he had first sat at his desk that morning, and not a page had he written that had not been scrapped.

It was a glorious summer's day, not a cloud in the sky. People thronged the streets and alleyways of the town dressed in their colourful summer clothes as the sun shone down on the world. He walked through the crowded streets, head down and shoulders hunched against the jostling mass of happy folk, seeing no-one in his miserable state of mind, until he came to the riverbank. Here he sat down in the shade of a big weeping willow, leaning back against its gnarled old trunk. His mind was racing, and he was beginning to panic.

He was close to despair. It had never been this difficult before. Everything he had written so far had flowed easily from his thoughts and translated into the written word with very little effort on his part. Occasional re-writes, grammar checks and editing - that was how it had been up to now.

What had gone wrong? Why could he not think of what to write next? He was under pressure to finish and present his new work within the next week. He had promised them; it should have been finished long before now. But he hadn't even started yet. What a mess! What on earth would happen if he didn't come up with the goods?

Time was running out fast. He stared moodily at the murky waters of the river. Swans and ducks with their families following behind paddled their way up and down stream, but he did not see them.

He saw nothing of the beauty surrounding him. His mind was filled with apprehension at his sudden loss of creative ability. What could he do? They would be so angry if he did not come up with a new idea very soon. Everyone was relying on him, and he had been so sure he could do it. There had never been any difficulties in the past, he was always ready on time.

And then there was the money; if he did not give them what they wanted in time he would not be paid. It was crucial for his survival that he earned the money soon. How on earth could he live on nothing?

Again he felt the panic beginning to take hold. He should have stayed with his family, not moved down here to the big city. He missed his wife so much, but she had been the one to convince him that he would be better off living and working where he could earn good money. And for a while she had proved right; everything had gone so well.

The thought of her at home in their little house brought a lump to his throat as he sat on the riverbank utterly miserable and dejected.

Since arriving in the city he had regularly sent what cash he could back to her, and returned intermittently to his home, which he loved. Due to pressure of work he could never stay for very long, but these visits were delightful and restorative. Always there were tears when he had to leave, but he travelled back to the city revitalised and recharged, ready to write again.

Except this time. He had been back now for a while,

but still no ideas had emerged, no inspiration from his Muse. Perhaps she had given up on him, who could tell? It was hopeless. He was doomed. If he stayed without producing the contracted work he would be in deep trouble, yet he could not return home a failure.

Feeling the tears begin to prickle his eyes, he abruptly stood up and stalked up and down at the river's edge. Nothing - absolutely nothing, not even the shadow of an idea. Kicking at the grass in his desperation he stared unseeing into the distance, walking in circles under the hanging branches of the old tree.

Frustrated and angry with himself he left the shade of the majestic old willow, marching quickly towards the nearest inn sign that he could see. A few glasses of real ale would help, he thought. At the very least he could drink his misery away for a while.

Three hours later he staggered back onto the street, full of bonhomie and drunken euphoria. The drink and the happy company had swept away his despair, temporarily at least. He lurched his way through the market square and on into the maze of side streets towards his rented room, smiling and waving at every passer-by. A party-like atmosphere pervaded the town under the blazing summer sun, with revellers dancing and singing their way along.

The strong drink took its toll before he reached his destination. Unable to focus and overwhelmed by sudden fatigue, he collapsed onto a wooden bench and slept the sleep of the dead in the heat of the afternoon. The sun blazed down on the sleeping writer as he snored away the summer's day, oblivious to the world and its problems.

When he finally tottered into his room it was dark. He had been asleep for hours on the bench out in the hot sun. The combination of a hangover and sunburn made him feel very unwell. He lay on his bed in the hope that he would sleep again, but it was not to be.

The room was spinning and he felt nauseous. What a terrible day - writer's block and now sickness. The drink-fuelled euphoria had long since passed and he began to shiver as his sunburned face added pain and discomfort to his feverish body. There was to be no relief for him that night. Feeling very ill he tried in vain to find a comfortable position on the bed.

It was a nightmare, nothing less. Wretchedly he tossed and turned on his narrow bed, drifting in and out of consciousness, demons and devils his sole companions in his misery. It was so hot in his room; he was bathed in sweat from head to toe, with no relief from his agony. There was not a breath of air on this sultry summer night, just humid discomfort for the restless young man.

The hours dragged slowly by as he suffered in the airless room, his body wracked by sickness and pain from his burned skin.

Finally, in the early hours of the morning as the dawn light filtered into his room, he fell into a deep sleep from sheer exhaustion. Now his dreams were somewhat quieter, less disturbed. From time to time he awoke, his thoughts jumbled. He meant to jot down his subconscious visions, but it was far too difficult to reach for his pen. Less restless now he slumbered on well into the new day.

When at last his eyes opened slowly and his thoughts cleared, he leapt from the bed with a shout of delight. Swaying from the sudden movement, his head throbbing like mad, he grabbed at his pen and sat down at his desk, waiting until his vision cleared and the hammers inside his brain stopped pounding.

He jotted down note after note as he recalled more of the night's dreams and nightmares. The idea for a new work was beginning to form itself in his mind. He was ecstatic; at last the characters began to take shape.

Images from his disturbed sleep ran again through his thoughts. Recalling what he could he wrote it down immediately. His thoughts turned to his friends here and back at home. In his mind he began to weave the story together, his fingers flying over the paper as he wrote.

He would use the dreams to begin with, and, interwoven with them, his good friends and their trades. Excitement and relief drove him on as he collated his thoughts and words. Headache and sunburn forgotten, the letters tumbled over the paper as he raced to put his new ideas into some kind of order.

There would be a weaver in the story; a carpenter, a joiner, a tinker and, yes, a tailor too! He laughed delightedly as he thought how pleased his friends would be to appear as characters in this new venture. Next he would add the entities he remembered from his disturbed sleep. He would use them all to form a brilliant new work.

At last he was ready, his notes finished, his idea crystal-clear in his mind. The wraith-like creatures, the mystical beings from his dreams and his friends from home; he would mix and mould them all into a stunning new creation. The world would be entranced.

The hot sun and the hours of drinking had combined to send him in the night glimpses of those magical creatures around which he would create his new masterpiece. He would be eternally grateful, despite the discomfort he had endured.

Bending his head over his desk, he began his work in earnest.

Based on his night's experiences, he knew at once what to call his new play.

Smiling now, young Will Shakespeare carefully wrote the chosen title at the top of a fresh piece of parchment.

'A MIDSUMMER-NIGHT'S DREAM'

TWINS

They were identical, like peas in a pod. Not a single person could tell them apart, not even their parents. The girls had enjoyed playing games over the years, changing places with each other and creating mayhem amongst their friends and family. As youngsters, if they had been dressed in different clothes to help with identification, they had simply swapped them and increased the confusion.

Nothing pleased them more than to be mistaken for each other, and the twins loved to watch the puzzled expressions on people's faces as they struggled to keep up with the girls' continual identity exchanges.

As they grew older the games subtly changed. The format was still the same, but now they had the most fun confusing their lovers. It was not unknown for some poor unsuspecting male to take one twin out to dinner and sleep with the other, totally unaware of the changeover. They shared every last intimate detail with each other, laughing at their own cleverness, and enjoying the subterfuge at the expense of their shared partners.

There was no shortage of admirers for the pretty girls. They wore their long dark hair in the same styles, either tumbling to their shoulders or pinned up to accentuate their beautifully long, elegant necks. Their smiling chocolate brown eyes wreaked havoc upon many a young man, and the sisters sailed happily on through life, determined to enjoy it to the full.

All through their university years they had worked hard and played hard, leaving in their wake a shoal of confused and embarrassed young men. Their lives revolved totally around each other, as they continued to dress alike and think alike. Pretty and clever, they were always surrounded by friends and admirers. The whole world was at their feet, the future bright.

They even shared their illnesses. Both had gone through the usual childhood measles, mumps and chicken-pox at the same time; now it was colds and flu. Always together, in sickness and in health.

Now in their early twenties, they worked as secretaries in the City of London. Although they shared a flat, they had decided that they should work for different companies, to avoid unnecessary confusion in the workplace. Their delight in changing places in their social life continued unabated, however. Many a man had been caught out by the two of them, although they did not always own up to the deceit. It had become a way of life, part of their joint existence - a delightful, but so far harmless, recreational pursuit.

Apart from the mortification felt by their victims, there was no real harm done as the years passed by and the girls kept on with their game.

They had decided to take a two-week holiday this year in Cyprus, staying in the popular resort of Paphos. Having totally confused the airline ground staff and cabin crew, much to the delight of the other passengers, the two girls disembarked from their flight into the hot sun of their chosen holiday island. Their arrival caused such a stir among the hotel staff that, having been shown to their room, they flopped down on their beds in hysterics at the perplexity they had left in their wake.

It set the scene for the next two weeks as, day after day, the pretty twins created havoc among locals and holidaymakers alike.

Dressed identically as usual, and with no distinguishing mark to help differentiate between them, the girls soon became the talk of the resort, reaching celebrity status within days of their arrival. They basked in the glory, continuing to tease and confuse the men falling over themselves to spend time with them. As always, their new conquests were treated in the same way as their past lovers, being moved around like chess pieces as the girls swapped back and forth without anyone noticing.

They sunbathed and swam in the warm blue sea, or in the hotel pool, lazing away the days and working on their tans. At night they went into the bustling town and spent their time at the bars and discos, which were always crowded well into the early hours of the mornings. Quick to make new friends, they soon joined a growing band of happy young holidaymakers from all over Europe simply out to enjoy their vacations to the full.

The problem arose when they both fell for the same man, a situation hitherto unknown to the twins. A handsome blue-eyed blond, and deeply tanned, he was from Sweden, working for the summer in one of the numerous small bars in Paphos. Unable to choose between the two girls, he took them out on the town in a threesome, drawing envious looks from the other hopefuls wishing desperately they could be in his place. They were a good-looking trio, two pretty girls with long dark hair and a handsome fair-haired young man to escort them.

The girls quickly lost interest in the group, preferring instead to be with their new admirer. No longer joining in with the fun and games arranged by their erstwhile friends, they stayed in the bar where the young Swede worked until he had finished his shift. Then it was time for the three of them to party together until dawn.

It was not long before the seemingly impossible happened. The twins began to experience a new emotion in their lives. A sharp word here, a scowl there. New territory for the sisters, always in unison before, never at odds about anything. Perfect symmetry, two halves of a whole.

But now it was different.

For the first time in their lives the twins began quarrelling and bickering when they were on their own. Each wanted to spend time alone with this sexy new acquaintance, and neither was prepared to allow the other the freedom to do so. It was stalemate. They had always shared their men; it was their way.

But not this time. Not this man.

When they were out with him they began to compete with each other, a totally new departure for them. Each girl strove to score verbal points over the other, delighting the young Swede as he revelled in their adulation. They were at each other's throats the whole time, so unlike their usual behaviour. The dark side of their normally sweet natures came to the fore, and the girls became aware for the first time of the violent effect that jealousy can have on a relationship.

Progressively their lives began to change in that hot, sunny climate. As tempers frayed, their unquestioning love for each other underwent its first real test. Beneath the cloudless blue sky the inseparable began to separate, little by little, imperceptibly at first, but the gap growing inexorably wider.

For the next six days and nights the twins fought and argued like children. Never before had they exchanged a cross word, now they were like enemies at war. Neither would give in over the young Swede. Each wanted him entirely to herself, resenting the other's presence, and it was dominating their lives.

They began to watch each other like hawks, ensuring that neither of them was able to slip away for a clandestine meeting with him. They had also started to wear different clothes; no more the identical outfits as always before. If one twin put her hair up, the other wore hers loose and flowing. Each made sure that, for the first time since they were born, they no longer appeared in public looking the same.

The split between them continued to widen almost daily, with feelings surfacing which neither had previously experienced. Their close-knit world was slowly falling apart. Spiteful comments and barbed remarks became the norm, each girl finding a totally unexpected depth of anger inside herself. Neither realised the extent of the damage being done to their close relationship, it was simply open warfare now.

The pretty sisters were too busy arguing and backbiting to notice when they passed the point of no return.

With only a couple of days of their holiday left, the girls were at loggerheads all the time. Continually spitting and snarling at each other, they had even come to blows over the young man.

Ever the gentleman, the object of their desires continued to behave impeccably towards each of them, silently acknowledging the problems he had created, but basking in the reflected glory. He loved to see the open envy of other men, and took great pains to treat both girls with equal amounts of affection and companionship.

There was, in truth, still nothing to choose between the two of them. They were mirror images of each other, beautiful, clever and sensual. He enjoyed taking them out together, their constant bickering causing him endless amusement.

When the accident happened, he was there with them. It was his quick reaction in calling the ambulance to the scene that enabled the paramedics to start work on the girls so quickly.

In the modern hospital at Larnaca, the twins' distraught parents, summoned from England by the hospital chief of staff, listened to the shaken young man as he recounted the story of the accident. They had all hired mopeds for the day, he told them as he had earlier informed the police. He had been taking them to see the ancient caves near Paphos. The girls had been very bad-tempered when they set out, arguing and shouting at one another. The day had been even hotter than usual, and the road out of town was dry and dusty.

On a particularly narrow stretch of the twisting mountain road he had been riding ahead of the girls, and had been unaware of the disaster unfolding behind him until he heard the screaming. As he braked hard and turned back to look, he could see that both girls had come off their bikes on a vicious bend in the road. One of them had managed to grab onto a small clump of coarse island grass as they both toppled over the edge of the precipice, and was screaming in terror as he raced back to her aid.

It was a particularly dangerous bend, with warning signs at intervals along the roadside. Unfortunately, the low metal fencing was no match for the weight of the falling sisters and their bikes, and had simply buckled under the impact.

The mopeds had careered over the edge, and as he rushed back to help he could see far below the mangled wreckage of the two small vehicles . . . and one body. Grabbing the screaming girl by the wrist just as the clump of grass uprooted from the sun-baked earth, he pulled her back up onto the road, and called the emergency services immediately on his mobile phone.

Helped by some passing British soldiers on leave from their base, he had tried to reach the other twin, but it had been too late.

He was so sorry, so very sorry, he told the sobbing parents. Everyone agreed that it was now vital to support the remaining twin through this harrowing time. For over twenty years the girls had been inseparable, like two halves of one person. She would be utterly devastated at the loss of her sister.

While she remained here in hospital they could watch

over her, but she would need counselling when she had recovered. Her family and friends would rally round to help, but the future for her would be incredibly hard without her identical twin.

The distraught parents sat by their daughter's bedside, holding her hand. She had been unconscious for a long time following the surgery on her injuries, some internal from the force of the impact, but the doctors were confident that she would recover totally.

Physically at least. Emotionally - who could tell?

For the twins' parents, the ultimate despair was the uncertainty. Which daughter had died, and which had survived? They could not yet be sure; even the young Swede did not know, and it simply added to their anguish. They reluctantly left the room for a short while as the day wore on, and the Swedish lad came in to sit with the patient, so that they could get themselves a cup of coffee.

He sat by the bedside holding the bandaged hand, his eyes full of tenderness and worry as he watched the still figure in the bed. What an appalling tragedy to befall these beautiful girls. How would this twin cope with the loss of her sister, her other half? He could not even imagine, but he would be there to help her, that was his whispered promise to her as she lay so still and fragile in her hospital bed. The girls had become very precious to him, and he would not walk away from this lovely young lady in her grief and shock.

He too wondered which of the two sisters had survived, and which had died. As usual on that awful day, they had still kept up their silly game of 'Who's Who', despite their angry words and arguments. What an appalling nightmare for everyone, to be so unsure. 'Life can be so very cruel,' he thought as he sat quietly with the injured girl.

As he dozed in the chair later in the day, the patient moved slightly, opening her eyes slowly as she regained consciousness. It took her a while to work out where she was, and even longer to recall what had happened. She was in a lot of pain, and gradually as her vision cleared, she looked around the hospital room until she focused on the young man sitting in the chair by the bed.

She smiled at the sight of him waiting there, despite her discomfort. 'He's simply gorgeous, well worth fighting for,' she thought to herself. There was a momentary knot in her stomach as she remembered the road to the caves, and the accident.

A moment's guilt, a tug on her heartstrings - quickly over, and hastily dismissed.

Gazing at the tanned and handsome young Swede, she experienced again the deep feelings of love that he had brought to her.

He was hers now. Hers alone. It was sad of course, very sad, but it had been necessary. Her sister would not give him up, she had wanted him for herself too.

Well, she was not going to have him, not now.

Her mind drifted back to the narrow, twisting mountain road, to their shouted arguments as they rode the mopeds up the steep slope. Her sister, her bloody sister - yelling at her that she'd never give him up, that she'd see her twin dead first. That had done it. The final straw; those fatal words.

She had reacted spontaneously; a moment's madness in the heat and dust of the summer afternoon. Without thinking, she had responded to the verbal abuse as she completely lost control of her temper.

It had not taken much to swerve her bike viciously at her sister's machine so that she veered off the road. He was riding ahead of them, he couldn't see what was happening. As the moped and its terrified rider slid sideways over the low barrier, she herself had fallen heavily off her own bike as its momentum took it over the cliff edge. Grabbing instinctively at a massive clump of grass as she fell, she hung there screaming for help, watching her sister and the bikes plummet like stones onto the rocks beneath.

As he came racing to her rescue, like a knight on a white charger, she knew that she had won. Even in her terror as she hung there, she knew that he would be hers now, locked in to her forever by the tragedy. Her moment of madness would, after all, give her what she so badly wanted.

Her thoughts racing as he pulled her to safety, despite the pain from her injuries, she realised in seconds that everyone would believe her to be inconsolable at the loss of her identical twin. She must play the part to perfection. They could never guess what had really happened on that mountain road.

Safe now in her hospital bed, watching her beloved young man as he dozed in the chair, her mind was working overtime. It was a tragedy, of course it was, but it would be her secret. No-one would ever know the truth, and she would receive sympathy and love for the rest of her life.

Even more important, she would never again have to share anything or anybody with her twin sister. Her shadow. Her other self. 'No, not any more,' she thought grimly.

He would be hers - for the first time in her life, hers alone. 100%, not 50/50. Not shared. Just . . . hers.

Smiling to herself, she closed her eyes. She liked the sound of that, very much indeed. Everything for herself in future. But for now, she must assume the role of the distraught twin. Time to become the grieving sister, finding solace and comfort in the love of her family and friends.

And a new life with the man for love of whom she had committed the ultimate perfect murder.

NEMESIS

Everything had gone according to plan. Poor Lady Marjorie had met with a fatal accident one morning whilst out riding and the whole village was in deep mourning.

The tragedy had devastated the entire community. Many of the villagers worked for Lady Marjorie's family on the estate, and their families before them. It was a tradition in the picturesque little hamlet. Everyone knew everyone else; it had seemed an idyllic existence until that fateful morning.

Everybody had turned out for the funeral that chilly spring day. The daffodils were in full bloom and the sun shone over the sad gathering at the graveside. The tiny church was full; Lady Marjorie had been very popular in the village. Such a kind lady, always ready to help those in need. She would be sorely missed.

Her husband, Sir Hugh, had led the mourners in the procession to the church, despite his anguish. None who saw him could help but feel sorry for the man. It was such a tragedy to befall the family, life was so unfair. How would he cope without his lovely wife? She had been at his side since their marriage in the same little church only nine short years before.

The couple lived in the Manor House on the hill, which had been in Sir Hugh's family for generations. Although there had been rumours of financial problems, they had seemed very happy together. So many of the big estates were proving too costly to run these days, but apart from the occasional cutback in staff, Sir Hugh and Lady Marjorie had been very careful to ensure that everyone had enough to eat and a roof over their heads. They had looked after the estate workers very well, but what would happen now that the mistress was no longer there to organise the running of the big house and its cottage industries?

Jim, the groom who had helped Lady Marjorie onto her horse that dreadful morning, could not stop the tears flowing. He stood in the church as the vicar led the funeral service, sobbing uncontrollably. He was not alone - hardly anyone there that day did not give way to their feelings. The servants from the Manor House stood together at the back of the church while the friends and family of the deceased sat in the ancient pews. Dressed in deep mourning black, the congregation shed many tears as they prayed for the soul of the much-loved lady.

It was a long, distressing day, every detail having been worked out with precision before the funeral. Lady Marjorie was buried in the family plot alongside Sir Hugh's ancestors under a magnificent yew tree that spread its branches out over the grave. A peaceful spot in the old graveyard, chosen for the family by a long-dead relative generations before.

Many of the mourners returned to the Manor House after the funeral, to give their support to the distraught widower. He broke down in tears from time to time, but the love and sympathy of friends and family carried him through that heartbreaking day.

As the evening shadows lengthened and the visitors departed, Sir Hugh dismissed the staff, telling them he would not require their services any further that day. He thanked them all for their love and support; he would be retiring early that night. They murmured their condolences, then sadly left him alone in the large and comfortable drawing room.

Alone at last, Sir Hugh poured himself a large whisky and stood pensively gazing out of the tall windows at the beautiful garden outside, where the last rays of the sun cast long shadows across the immaculate lawns. His shoulders were hunched, the very picture of a grieving husband as he stood staring out at his shattered world.

There was a discreet tap on the door, and Sir Hugh turned to see the village schoolteacher, Anne Laidlaw, slip into the room. She paused by the door, not sure whether to approach him or not. Smiling with delight, he held out his arms to her and she rushed across the room into his embrace. They held each other tightly and she lifted her face to his kisses.

He assured her that they would not be disturbed by the staff. She had not been seen entering the house, so they were able to talk freely. They could hardly contain their joy at being alone together. Sir Hugh once more confirmed his love for the schoolteacher, and they quietly talked through their plans for their future together.

When it had become obvious to Sir Hugh over the previous months that his feelings for Anne were far deeper than he could ever have anticipated, and that she returned his love, something had to be done. He no longer loved his wife; he wanted to be free to live his life with the teacher. The lovers had schemed together, plotting the demise of the lovely lady who had remained blissfully ignorant of their cold-blooded plans.

It had been very easy, after all. Lady Marjorie always went riding in the mornings, and took the same route through the forest on the estate. Her husband had simply left the house before her and hidden himself behind one of the huge old trees, waiting for her to ride by.

As his wife's hunter had approached at a trot he had leapt out from behind the old oak tree brandishing a broken branch which he slashed backwards and forwards under the horse's head, shouting and yelling. Terrified by the sudden attack, the animal had reared up and thrown Lady Marjorie backwards onto the ground before galloping off into the forest. She had landed on her back with such force that her neck had snapped, killing her instantly.

Sir Hugh had raced back to the Manor House so that he was in his study when the stable lads rushed in with the news of the accident. He was, of course, utterly heartbroken, devastated at the news. As he joined his employees at the scene of the disaster, his deep distress was evident for all to see. Shaking their heads in sympathy and shock, they could tell that the Master would never recover from the tragic death of his beautiful, saintly wife.

There was no suspicion of any relationship between him and the schoolteacher as they had been extremely discreet all these months. It was imperative that no-one had any idea that the fatal accident had been caused deliberately; they knew only too well that their future together depended on that.

The callous lovers planned to go away together after a decent period of mourning. Next month they would embark on a cruise, booked and paid for by Sir Hugh on his last visit to London, safe in the knowledge that by the time the ship sailed, his wife would surely be dead. The tickets were already in his safe, their passport to paradise.

As the days passed slowly after the funeral, the village began to return to normal. Sir Hugh had made it known to the world that he was still so deeply traumatised by the death of his wife that he had decided to undertake a long sea voyage in order to recover his spirits. Everyone agreed that he needed to get away for a while, his gaunt face and loss of weight bearing testament to his deep grief.

Anne Laidlaw had also made arrangements to be absent from the school for a week or two, on the pretext of visiting her ailing parents in Scotland.

There was absolutely nothing to link the two of them, so nobody noticed that they would both be away at the same time.

The crowds on the dockside cheered and waved back at the passengers crowding the rails on board the magnificent ship as she pulled away at the start of her voyage. The brass bands on the quay and on deck played their hearts out as a party atmosphere enveloped the passengers and their friends and families left behind. A few tears were shed, but overall it was a joyous occasion.

As the weak April sunshine broke through the clouds the two lovers hugged each other in the grandeur of their first-class stateroom on board the huge ocean-going liner. They had each begun their journey that morning, and now it felt as if they were on their honeymoon. Arriving separately at the docks, they had met in their magnificent stateroom only after the ship had sailed.

There was nothing to stop them now that his wife was dead. They would, of course, have to wait a while before they could marry, but this voyage would give them time to be together away from the village, and to enjoy each other to the full. Their future was assured and they drank to each other in chilled champagne as the ship sailed out into the open sea.

The sun glinted on the polished mahogany of the massive decks, the burnished brass rails and the gleaming white paintwork of the liner. She was the proud new flagship of the line, a magnificent monument to man's achievements. Undoubtedly the finest ship ever to be built anywhere in the world.

As she headed for the horizon her name was clearly visible high up on her bow.

The lovers, with not a single thought for his poor dead wife, continued their celebrations in the luxurious surroundings, lost in each other's company and blissfully oblivious to the world outside their door. Wrapped up in their own little world, Lady Marjorie lay forgotten in her grave as they happily plotted their future together.

Gathering speed now as she set out on her maiden voyage, the mighty RMS TITANIC steamed her way out across the vast ocean, and on into history . . .

FIVE SIXTEEN

The family had gathered around her bed. It was a cold November day but the room was warm and cosy, a log fire burning brightly in the grate. The old lady lay as still as a statue in the snowy white sheets. She had been ill for so long; it was only a matter of time now.

Dr. Andrews looked down at her with a fond smile on his face. She had been his patient for almost 30 years, a feisty old bird but a genuinely good human being. She had become impatient with the world as she grew older and weaker, though she was still the esteemed family matriarch. She was loved by them all, each generation holding its own favourite memories of her in their hearts.

'The old dear's holding on for something,' he thought. Through all the pain and anguish of the long illness she had made it clear that her one remaining wish was to die with dignity. Looking around at the small group he acknowledged to himself that she could have wished for no better end, surrounded by her loved ones.

She should have slipped away days ago but something was holding her back. Defiant as always, she had maintained that she wouldn't go until the time was right, however ill she became.

There had been no movement from the bed for the last two days. It seemed impossible that she was still alive, but the old lady was still with them. Her son, grey-haired now himself, bent down to kiss her wrinkled face. He loved his mother dearly, as did everyone in the family, and he just wanted her to slip quietly away to her rest after all the suffering.

His wife sat by the bedside holding the tiny bird-like hand in hers, stroking that dear face as the minutes ticked by. Dawn was still some hours away and the men and women murmured quietly together as they maintained their vigil. She had earned their respect as well as their love; they would stay with her until the end.

What was she waiting for? Her son smiled down at his dear old mum. He knew her so well. St. Peter would have to wait until she was ready for him. Mercifully deep in the coma, she was finally free from the awful pain and discomfort of the last few months. They were all grateful for that at least.

As silence descended on the room there was a sudden cry from the bed, piercing through the stillness of the early hours. Everyone jumped at the unexpected noise and turned immediately to look at the little old lady lying there. They were amazed to see that her eyes were open and that she was smiling.

Her mouth was moving as her son bent over her to hear what she was trying to say. He could not make any sense of what he heard, just the few words . . . 'here,' 'safe,' and 'go now.' As he looked anxiously up at the doctor, his mother let out a long sigh and closed her eyes, still smiling.

Dr. Andrews took her fragile wrist gently in his hand, held it for a while then turned to face the family, speaking quietly and reverently.

'She's gone, I'm afraid. Totally peaceful though, you saw for yourselves. The struggle's over, she's at rest.'

The tears began then as the family members took it in turns to bend over old Martha Jane and kiss her gently as she took her leave. Dr. Andrews looked at his watch.

Time of death . . . . 5.16 a.m.

Twelve thousand miles away in Auckland, New Zealand,

a tiny human being slithered into the world. Her exhausted mother sank back on her pillows as the midwife gathered up the minute bundle and checked her over. The baby began to bawl loudly as the new mother and father hugged each other with delight, tears of joy coursing down their cheeks.

Little Martha Jane had finally arrived. A much longed-for baby, her entrance into the world was the answer to her parents' prayers. She was to be named after her mother's great-grandmother over in England, as a thank-you for everything the kind old lady had done for her family over the years.

It was a hot summer's day in Auckland and the labour had been long and hard. It didn't matter now; the tiny child was here safe and well, announcing her arrival with a lusty pair of lungs.

Her joyful parents knew they must telephone England at once with news of her birth. Old Martha Jane had been ill for a very long time, and the confirmation of her great-great-granddaughter's arrival would cheer her up.

The new father checked the time of birth with the doctor. 6.16 p.m. He picked up the phone on the bedside table, smiling down at his wife and brand-new baby daughter as he dialled the number.

It would be the early hours of the morning in England, so he must get this right. New Zealand was 13 hours ahead of the U.K.

Martha Jane had arrived at precisely - yes, that was right, he'd got it right.

Time of birth . . . .5.16 a.m.

THE NECKLACE

Set on a black velvet stand in the centre of the jeweller's window, it sparkled and glowed in the sunlight, radiating a halo of rainbows around itself and attracting the attention of passers-by. Shimmering and dancing on the velvet backdrop the necklace drew gasps of amazement from the window shoppers.

She saw it as she crossed the road and her heart leapt into her throat. Captivated by its sheer beauty she stood breathlessly mesmerised, staring through the window. She had never seen anything like it before. The stones looked as though they were made of ice. The tiny crystals caught the rays of the sun through the glass and reflected them back a hundredfold. The necklace seemed to move as the lights danced around it, a magnificent centrepiece for the display window.

She stood motionless, her nose pressed up against the glass, hardly daring to breathe. It was so beautiful; a four-strand choker necklace. It seemed to have a life of its own as it twinkled and shone on the stand.

There was no price tag on it. She thought it would be far beyond her means, but it was just so very pretty. She would love to have it, to wear it to the Summer Ball next week. Her long dress was luxurious dark blue velvet, and she had been searching for a choker necklace to set it off.

Now she had found it, but could she afford it?

Nervously she entered the shop, glancing back at the shimmering crystals in the window. As the shop assistant came across and asked if he could help her, she took a deep breath and asked to see the necklace on the black velvet stand.

The assistant smiled and carefully unlocked the sliding partition at the back of the window. He gently removed the stand and placed it on the glass counter top. Under the shop strip-lights the beautiful piece of jewellery sparkled and twinkled even more, rainbows shimmering all around it. She caught her breath as she looked longingly at it, her hand flying to her throat as she mentally pictured how it would look there.

She held out her hand and gently touched the tiny crystal beads. Four rows of perfectly matching stones the size of teardrops, and a silver filigree clasp at the back. Stunning. Simple and magnificent. As she ran her fingers over the crystals the assistant asked if she would like to try it on.

Of course she would! He undid the clasp and carefully removed the necklace from its stand. She held up her long blonde hair so that he could put it around her neck, and as he fastened it in place she looked into the mirror on the countertop. The people in the shop heard her gasp and turned to look.

It was perfect. She flushed with pleasure as she listened to the comments from the customers and staff. The necklace could have been made for her. The crystals shone against her fair skin, the long blonde hair providing a backdrop of perfection. She simply had to have it, whatever the cost.

As she discussed the price with the helpful assistant, he regaled her with the story of the necklace. It had come to them from an aristocrat living in the highlands of Scotland, he told her. He had originally bought it from an elderly Russian émigré, who had warned him that the stones were considered unlucky, cursed even. Intrigued, the Scottish Duke had listened to the tale of the crystals.

The Russian had told him that the perfect matching

stones had been stolen from the Imperial Winter Palace in St. Petersburg the night Tsar Nicholas and his family were assassinated at Ekaterinburg, back in 1918. They had belonged to the youngest daughter, one of the Grand Duchesses, and were to be have been made into a necklace for her by the Court jeweller. The wretched thief had instead sold them to another jeweller in St. Petersburg, who had created this beautiful necklace from the pretty gems.

Legend had it that the evil monk Rasputin had procured the stones for the Grand Duchess, enough by itself to damn the lovely jewels. He had been reviled throughout Russia for his domination of the Tsarina and her family, and the rumour that he himself had given the tiny crystal teardrops to the Grand Duchess had started the story many years before.

The old man went on to tell the Duke that the first two owners of the choker had met with sudden unexplained deaths. Two young women, both found dead in mysterious circumstances; one in St. Petersburg, the other in Moscow. There had never been an explanation for their deaths; both had been attributed to natural causes. The only link between the two, tenuous in the extreme, had been ownership of the crystal necklace. Folklore had created the story that the stones were cursed, belonging as they had to the murdered Grand Duchess, and linked by history and rumour to the dreaded Rasputin.

The second of the victims had been his sister, he had sadly told the young Scot. When the old man had fled from the Revolutionary madness enveloping his beloved country, he had taken with him only a few items that were easy to carry and to sell. The crystal necklace had been among those items.

The old Russian earnestly warned the Duke about the supposed history of the stones, but he was not a superstitious man. He laughed off the story; it was simply a beautiful piece of jewellery, how could it possibly have anything to do with the sad deaths of two of its owners? He was sure that it was simply coincidence. Legends grow as they are repeated over the years, and anything with a connection to the assassinated Royal Family or the evil Rasputin would naturally engender such gossip.

His young wife would adore the necklace. A beautiful and much-loved lady, he would surprise her with this very special gift. The Duke comforted the old émigré, thanking him for his concern and assuring him that he believed the myth to be simply that, nothing more.

Reluctantly, the old man had sold the necklace to the Scottish aristocrat. He was desperately in need of money, but he had felt that the Duke should know the story surrounding the jewels. A proud man, the old émigré had left the magnificent necklace with the young Scot, uneasy in his mind but knowing that he had at least warned him about the legend of the crystals. They were all he had left to sell; he had no choice.

The young Scottish Duchess had been utterly enchanted by her gift. She had worn the necklace just once, for a Grand Ball held in the castle ballroom. It had been admired by everyone attending the Ball, and she had been the centre of attention all evening. Her young husband had decided against telling her the story relayed to him by the elderly Russian; there had been no point.

Later that same night the Duke had found his wife lying on her bed, cold to his touch. She had retired alone to her room, tired but happy after her wonderful evening, while he was saying goodnight to his guests. Frantically he had called his servants to her side, and the doctor had been summoned immediately. But it had been too late - there was nothing anyone could do to help her.

She had died alone in her room, with no apparent cause of death. He was heartbroken as he sat on the bed with her, sobbing uncontrollably until his valet gently helped him up and took him away from his beloved young wife's body. The doctor sedated him but his grief was dreadful to behold.

The pretty young Duchess had still been dressed in her ballgown and wearing the necklace when the Duke had found her.

Griefstricken, he had recalled the words of the elderly Russian. Could there after all be any truth in the legend of the gemstones? Too shocked by the loss of his young wife to make any sense of her death, he had given the necklace to one of the trusted servants and told her to get rid of it at once.

That was how the jeweller had come by the lovely crystal choker.

The assistant felt that the young woman should know about the story, but she could not believe that there could be anything sinister about this beautiful piece of craftsmanship. It was simply a tale created around the stones, and it had grown over the years. Russian folklore, nothing more, embellished each time it was repeated. A myth created around the tragic Russian Royal Family and their brutal murders, and enhanced by the inclusion of Rasputin's name.

She wanted this necklace above all else; it was her dream to own such a magnificent piece of jewellery. After much discussion, she eventually agreed to pay the asking price, using up virtually all her savings but determined to have the beautiful jewels. She almost danced out of the shop with her precious crystals wrapped in an elegant satin-lined red leather box.

She was thrilled to be the new owner of the choker. A level-headed girl, she was also convinced that the story of the necklace was undoubtedly a fabrication, created to add an air of intrigue and mystery. 'Probably just to add to the price,' she thought wryly.

On the night of the Summer Ball she carefully applied her makeup and dressed slowly as her excitement grew. The blue velvet ballgown was perfect for her colouring. The low neckline demanded a special piece of jewellery to complete the picture. And she had the most perfect necklace to set it all off.

Dressed in the sumptuous velvet, her hair shining and sweeping her shoulders, she stood in front of the mirror admiring her reflection.

Now for the final touch, the pièce de résistance. She reached for the crystal necklace and carefully slid it around her neck. With trembling fingers she did up the clasp, and stood back to survey the effect. It was startling. She looked stunning. The choker set off her fair skin and blonde hair to perfection, glittering around her throat and highlighting the blue velvet ballgown.

She was ecstatic, breathless with excitement and anticipation. Never in her life had she looked so beautiful. She would be the Belle of the Ball. Tonight would be the best night of her life. The crystal choker glowed and sparkled in the bedroom light.

Twirling round and dancing across the floor, she laughed with delight. Her cheeks were flushed; she had never been so happy. Trying to calm herself down, she made herself stand still once more in front of the full-length mirror, searching for any tiny detail which needed attention.

There was nothing - it was all totally perfect. A dream come true.

But as she steadied herself, checking her dress, her hair, every single inch of herself, and revelling in her appearance, something strange seemed to be happening to the mirror. Puzzled, she stared at her reflection. The glass appeared to be rippling in the light. She gasped, becoming a little frightened as the image staring back at her seemed to alter. Imperceptibly, a subtle change came over the reflected face in the mirror.

The face of a young woman seemed to superimpose itself upon that of her own. Similar to herself, very pretty with long blonde hair, and wearing the same necklace.

It looked like her, but it was not her. Unable to look away she stared transfixed as the face looking back at her smiled sadly. Trembling now, she watched the image shake its lovely head as it began to fade, to be replaced by her own face once more.

She blinked hard, trying to stop herself shaking. 'How stupid. Utterly ridiculous. It must be nerves,' she thought, as she peered into the mirror, seeing no-one but herself. She must be over-excited at the prospect of a wonderful evening ahead. An optical illusion undoubtedly, possibly due to the crystals shining so brightly and being reflected back from the glass.

Of course. Simply an illusion. She must calm herself down, it would be a long night, a splendid night. Smiling, she performed another twirl in front of the long mirror and turned to pick up her blue velvet evening bag from the dressing table. Glancing back quickly over her shoulder, she reassured herself that it was her own reflection in the mirror, and smiled at her earlier stupidity.

The necklace had grown a little tight around her neck, she noticed. Perhaps she had fastened the clasp onto the wrong link. It needed a slight adjustment. As she reached up under her hair to undo the catch, she became aware of an uncomfortable pressure around her throat.

The crystal choker seemed to be slowly and inexplicably tightening around the pale skin of her neck. She began to panic, telling herself that she was imagining it, but as she reached under her hair to loosen the clasp the pressure increased. Clawing now at the silver filigree with her fingers, however hard she tried, she could not undo it. As her panic increased she began to pull at the strands, trying desperately to ease the pressure on her throat.

It was hopeless. Twisting and turning in her attempts to break the necklace she was becoming breathless as her fear turned to terror. The crystals bit deep into her skin as they tightened their grip. She was crying now, sobbing in frightened desperation. She tried to call out for help as her voice grew fainter, but there was nobody to hear her or help her.

With a relentless power of its own the choker grew ever tighter, tighter, inexorably closing her throat in its grip. As her breathing became harsher and she struggled to rip the crystals from her neck an onrushing darkness began to envelop her.

She felt herself falling, her mind racing even at the height of her terror. Through the black mist blurring her eyes and her thoughts came the stark realisation that the beautiful crystal necklace WAS evil; cursed, as she had been warned.

Dear God, the story had been true.

The face . . . the face she had seen in the mirror. It must have been the young Scottish Duchess who had died so tragically. Trying to warn her, to help her.

But it was too late . . . too late.

Struggling desperately against the black tide rushing over her, her last thought, as she finally succumbed to the pressure of the stones, struck home with startling clarity.

It was the necklace, the necklace itself. Her beautiful crystal choker had been responsible for the other deaths; the three young women who had owned it before.

Too late now, she knew the truth; the dreadful, fatal truth. They had all been strangled by the pretty crystals. Rasputin's evil legacy.

Now it was her turn.

As she fell to the floor, her breathing stilled for ever by the pressure around her neck, the four strands of crystal teardrops slowly unwound and slid onto the carpet.

There was not a mark on her skin. Not a single trace of the fatal grip of the jewels on her throat.

Sparkling and shimmering in the light, the necklace lay where it fell. A superb piece of craftsmanship, so beautiful to look at.

In time it would find its way back into a jeweller's shop window somewhere, to captivate yet another buyer.

But for now it would remain beside the body of its latest victim.

Waiting . . .

THE DINNER PARTY

The Dowager Duchess took her place at the head of the table and bowed graciously to her guests. They all sat down in their assigned seats, admiring the resplendent dinner table laid with the family Royal Doulton china and highly-polished silver crested tableware on a beautiful hand-embroidered cloth. The Duchess was renowned for her dinner parties; she employed the best cook in London whose reputation for producing the most wonderful food was justly earned.

Set in the centre of the huge dining room the antique table and chairs provided a superb spectacle for the guests as they appreciatively gazed upon the opulence of the cut crystal glasses, the magnificent table decorations, the gleaming family silverware and fine porcelain china.

The room was full of exquisite floral arrangements, heavily scenting the air. Everyone was attired in evening dress, as befitted the occasion. The ladies wore their best long gowns and jewellery, and the gentlemen looked extremely dapper in their smart black suits, white silk shirts and black bow ties. It was a very select gathering, and the evening promised to be extremely enjoyable for everyone.

The Duchess herself was just a teensy bit apprehensive at the moment, however. Her butler and maid were both off sick with the flu, so she had borrowed two staff members from her good friend, Lady Ffortescue (with two ff's.) Unfortunately, they had only recently joined the Ffortescue household and were still learning their trade. Still, it was the best that she could do at such short notice, and she was sure the magnificent meal

Mrs. Bates had prepared would automatically overcome any shortcomings on the part of the borrowed staff.

Delighted with the appearance of the large room, and the splendour of her table settings, she settled down to enjoy the evening with her party of eleven very distinguished guests.

As the conversation round the table grew more animated and everyone began to relax over their first glass or two of wine, the Dowager Duchess signalled to her temporary butler to bring in the delicious homemade soup, one of Mrs. Bates' specialities. She noticed for the first time that Sir Montague Pugh's face was a trifle red above his magnificent handlebar moustache, and wondered vaguely how many whiskies the old boy had already imbibed. A notorious drinker, he was nonetheless a superb raconteur, and was invited to many dinner parties on the strength of his tale-telling alone.

She watched with delight as Mr. Bates and the young maid entered the dining room, serene in the knowledge that this was to be one of her very, very best dinner parties.

Unfortunately, it all started to go wrong with the first course. Trying to hold the huge china soup tureen and ladle the lobster bisque into Lord Henry's Royal Doulton bowl had proved too much for the nervous young maid, Rose. She had tipped some of the hot pink liquid into his Lordship's lap, and, totally disconcerted by her own clumsiness and his sudden anguished yelp of pain, she had stepped back and tripped over the exquisite Axminster rug. As the tureen hurtled to the floor showering the nearest diners with hot soup, Dr. Marcus, the eminent London gynaecologist, had raced off to the kitchen for wet cloths to mop up the mess.

Lord Henry abruptly shot upright up as his groin area was dowsed in molten hot liquid, knocking his glass of red wine onto the snow-white tablecloth. As the deep red puddle spread over the pristine linen, Sir Montague

Pugh let forth a mighty guffaw, causing his near neighbours to jump. Chuckling to himself as his Lordship rubbed away at his lap with his napkin, the old reprobate poured himself another glass of wine while the other diners attempted to behave as though nothing had happened and continued with their conversations.

The Duchess was utterly mortified, but was rapidly assured by the victims that they were absolutely fine, apart from the odd soup stain on their clothing, and that no real harm had been done. Lord Henry, still a tad damp around his nether regions, resumed his seat with the proverbial British 'stiff upper lip', and Sir Montague continued to empty and refill his glass with impeccable precision.

Rose was pacified by the assembled company with soothing noises and quiet sympathy, but it was obvious from her white face that she was now totally overawed by the whole occasion, if she hadn't been before. She would undoubtedly now find it extremely difficult to continue with her duties, especially with the Dowager Duchess glaring at her, but there was nothing else she could do. Taking a few deep breaths she stood behind the unnerved hostess, awaiting her next duty.

All spillages now successfully mopped up, the twelve diners settled down once more to regain their breath.

The next course was a whole Scottish salmon, cooked to perfection by Mrs. Bates and laid on a silver salver, garnished with slices of lime and lemon, atop a bed of watercress. By now, with the soup course just a memory, everyone was more than ready to enjoy the beautifully-presented fish, salivating as the aroma from the platter reached their nostrils. Mr. Short, the 'borrowed' butler, served the guests as a trembling Rose attempted to clear away the unused soup bowls and spoons, and return them to the kitchen.

Everyone held their breath as she staggered out of the

room balancing the twelve porcelain dishes, then relaxed as the door swung to behind her. As the conversation began again and the salmon was dispatched with relish, Rose reappeared in the dining room, a little flushed but with relief showing clearly on her face. She had negotiated the walk to the kitchen without dropping a single bowl or soup spoon.

Still unnerved by her experience with the Lobster Bisque, but steadily gaining in confidence, she helped Mr. Short clear away the plates when everyone had finished the delicious salmon. Sadly, her confidence was short-lived. As she carried an armful of plates and cutlery out of the door the bow at the back of her apron strings caught on the door handle, jerking her backwards as she walked.

The guests jumped at her sudden shriek, followed by the crash of breaking china as it hit the floor. Accompanied by the crested silverware, twelve Royal Doulton plates tumbled to the ground to form a great mosaic composed of hundreds of pieces as Rose stood with her head in her hands, shaking like a leaf.

The Dowager Duchess sat immobile in her chair, her face frozen in disbelief, while the guests began muttering to each other or downing more liquid refreshments. Mr. Short shot out into the hall to assist in the clearing-up process, aided by a furious Mrs. Bates who had emerged from the kitchen at the sound of the fracas, wielding her broom like a modern-day Boadicea. The assembled company was struggling to maintain the status quo but it was becoming obvious that this was *not* going to be one of the Duchess's better evenings.

The Lady herself was trying desperately to continue as though nothing had happened, apologising profusely to all her guests and calling upon every ounce of her gilded upbringing to handle the situation with aplomb. Her companions talked among themselves, keeping the conversation flowing as though nothing untoward had occurred, with Sir Montague racing to the rescue with one of his noted stories to keep everyone amused.

Mrs. Bates appeared in the doorway looking very flushed, followed closely by Mr. Short. Rose had retired for the moment, collapsed in a chair in the kitchen. The main course, comprising a magnificent sirloin of beef with many dishes of vegetables was safe in the hands of the cook and the butler . . .or so it seemed.

The Duchess had by now drunk a little more than her customary three glasses of wine as she tried valiantly to keep up her conversation with the American Ambassador and the Secretary of State for Health. With one eye on the butler and cook as they served the guests with the beef and accompaniments, she began to relax a little as her fellow diners murmured appreciatively at the wondrous array of food on their plates. Not one of them seemed to have noticed that the Duchess's tiara was slightly off-centre.

Mrs. Bates sighed with relief as the guests began to tuck into her sumptuous repast. She smiled nervously at the Duchess, who smiled back, both women on edge and close to screaming point, but determined that the evening should be a success despite the disasters. Mr. Short, with a final glance behind him, saw that all was in order and the celebrated ensemble was tucking in to Mrs. Bates' wonderful roast beef. He followed the plump cook back to the kitchen where Rose sat crumpled and tearful in the chair.

Muttering soothing noises to her, and chivvying her along, the two older servants began to prepare the final course, a splendid Bombe Surprise. Mrs. Bates was adamant that Mr. Short should carry the heavy lidded silver dish into the dining room. Rose could help serve the guests, but she was not to be trusted with the mighty dessert. She could assist in the clearing away of the used plates and cutlery after the roast beef, then they would wait the customary ten minutes while everybody at the table chatted and digested the delicious main course.

Copious amounts of wine had already been consumed, on top of the glasses of sherry before dinner, and the Duchess had provided magnums of Moet et Chandon champagne to accompany the Bombe.

Sir Montague was beginning to be a bit of a worry, as he became more and more inebriated by the minute. His arms waving wildly as he chattered and laughed raucously, the old boy had become something of a loose cannon at the meal table. His immediate neighbours had a wild, helpless look in their eyes as they struggled to maintain their impeccable manners in the face of the onslaught, deafened by his booming voice and extremely disconcerted as his arms flailed about dangerously close to their faces.

His poor hostess, still trying desperately to keep up appearances, was becoming more unhinged by the second. The strain of keeping an eye on Sir Montague and attempting to cope with Rose's nerve-wracking behaviour was taking its toll, and her hand was shaking as she lifted yet another glass of wine to her lips.

In spite of her shattered nerves, Rose helped Mr. Short to take the used Royal Doulton plates and the crested silverware to the kitchen without further mishap. The staff watched the clock, and when the ten minutes were up, Mrs. Bates pushed three sparklers into the huge dessert and Mr. Short lit them. It was ready. The butler picked up the heavy dish and began the short journey to the dining room. Rose held the door open for him and Mrs. Bates sank into her chair with a sigh of relief, mopping her face with her pinafore.

Unfortunately for her and the waiting guests the relief was a trifle premature . . .

Duke, the Duchess's huge black Labrador, had been asleep in his basket next to the kitchen range during the proceedings. He lazily opened his eyes and blinked slowly, as Mr. Short started through the door towards the dining room carrying the heavy silver dish. As Rose held the door open Duke, sensing freedom, stretched himself and before anyone could stop him, shot through the open door as Mr. Short arrived at the dining room.

The momentum of the big dog's charge carried him across the hallway and straight into the back of Mr. Short's legs. The butler, with the weight of the heavy animal propelling him forwards, hurtled into the room desperately trying to hold onto the sparkling Bombe. The guests turned as one, mouths open in astonishment, to see the poor man's frantic efforts to maintain his balance as Duke slid across the polished floor taking Mr. Short's legs from under him.

Everyone froze as though in a tableau, watching the entangled duo. Mr. Short did not stand a chance. He fell seemingly in slow motion, and all eyes turned to the silver dish and cover as they flew out of his hands through the air.

The Bombe Surprise and its three spitting sparklers landed heavily in the middle of the table. The dish hit the American Ambassador on the head laying him out cold while the cover continued its flight, coming to rest with a thump against the beautiful candelabra centrepiece and knocking it over.

Sir Montague Pugh, puce in the face and snorting with laughter, fell sideways off his chair, creating a domino effect along the length of the table. His fellow guests were toppled off their chairs onto the best Axminster rug, landing heavily on top of each other as the room erupted into total bedlam.

As the party of diners attempted to collect themselves, to the accompaniment of hysterical booming laughter from Sir Montague, now rolling about on the floor with his felled victims, the dessert exploded like a real bomb, spraying the entire assembly with pieces of meringue and ice-cream. The sparklers were drowned in the flood of wine issuing from the overturned bottles, hissing loudly and emitting a disgusting smell of rotten eggs.

The poor Dowager Duchess turned pale and, her eyes crossed in her state of nerves, gracefully fainted face forwards onto the table, her tiara hanging off over one ear.

Pandemonium reigned. Mr. Short watched in horror from the floor as the five huge candles in the candelabra toppled onto the table and set fire to the decorations. Several other guests ran out of the room screaming blue murder, leaving Dr. Marcus to tend to his hostess and the American Ambassador. Sir Montague Pugh, prostrate with laughter and totally unable to move from the floor, was left there on his back with arms and legs waving feebly in the air, like a monstrous overgrown puppy.

As the felled diners picked themselves up off the floor and joined in the general melee, the Duchess remained thankfully oblivious to the drama as she lay unconscious, snoring gently with her head resting on the table.

Rose and Mrs. Bates rushed into the room as the noise level grew, standing in stupefied horror at the scene unfolding in the once-pristine dining room. As the blaze caught hold the gentlemen took off their jackets, trying desperately to douse the flames, unfortunately now being fuelled by the after-dinner brandy and liqueurs gurgling out of the overturned bottles.

The ladies stood in the hall twittering or weeping, the Countess of Ascot being the only one to have the presence of mind to dial 999, requesting the Fire Brigade and an ambulance.

Luckily for everyone struggling in the dining room, during renovations to the Georgian house a few months before, a state-of-the-art sprinkler system had been installed. As the flames licked up towards the ceiling, despite the best efforts of the valiant men battling the conflagration, the sprinkler system swung into action deluging everyone and everything in the room with freezing cold water. Swiftly extinguishing the fire the water continued to pour from the sprinkler heads, soaking the entire room and its contents.

Sir Montague's reaction was immediate. Bellowing at the top of his voice as the icy cold water hit him, he hauled himself up off the floor and lumbered drunkenly towards the door, unfortunately tripping over the sodden Duke who was cowering and whimpering under one of the chairs. Sprawling flat on his face once again, the irate knight lashed out at the big dog, which retaliated in its panic. Locked in combat like a pair of all-in wrestlers, the two rolled around on the soaked carpet, Duke snapping and biting as Sir Montague tried hard to throttle the big crazed animal.

Above the din the wailing of a siren could be heard in the distance as the local Fire Brigade raced in the direction of the Duchess's home.

It would be unkind to dwell on the events of the next few hours. The Dowager Duchess was taken by ambulance to a private hospital a few miles from her house, together with the American Ambassador. Apart from concussion, he had no serious injuries and was discharged the next morning.

The Duchess, however, remained closeted in her hospital room, distraught and inconsolable.

At the first opportunity she would leave for her mansion in the country, retreat from public life and try to put this horrendous occasion behind her - Prozac permitting.

The remaining guests, smoke-blackened and soaking wet, sadly made their way to their own homes. Sir Montague, nursing teeth marks about his person from his wrestling match with Duke, and uttering oath after oath in his booming voice, left the house with his luxuriant moustache drooping like a down-turned horseshoe. His temper and his language both equally foul, he struggled into the waiting taxi a sodden, bitten and very, very drunken wreck; a veritable bastion of British aristocracy.

The dining room was in need of very serious redecoration and the antique table had suffered badly in the fire. The room was a total shambles, but apart from that there were no unresolvable problems resulting from the evening's debacle apart from the poor Duchess's wounded pride. The ruined room could be restored in good time, and the shattered nerves of the guests showed only in their reluctance to accept further dinner invitations for the time being, at least.

Rose, poor Rose, never regained what little confidence she might have had. She now works behind the counter in Woolworth's, a job much more suited to the youngster's capabilities. Mr. Short immediately went into retirement, and currently looks after his allotment full time.

Mrs. Bates remains in the service of the Duchess, but, as there seems to be no sign of her employer holding another dinner party in the foreseeable future, she has resigned herself to cooking mundane meals for her employer and the staff at the mansion in the country.

She misses the glory days of London, but the memories of that dreadful evening return periodically to haunt her. Her beautiful Bombe Surprise - so lovingly sculpted - so painstakingly prepared. No-one in the dining room that night would ever again be able to face that particular dessert without frightful memories, and Mrs. Bates herself, a fiercely proud woman, will never, *never* again prepare such a magnificent finale to a meal. She simply could not bring herself to do so; she has the mental picture of that awful evening firmly embedded in her mind.

'Fancy all that work goin' to waste,' she muttered to herself. 'That bloody dog; always a nuisance Duke was.

Took a fair few chunks out of Sir Montague that night, though.' She grinned at the memory of the two of them rolling around on the carpet as the dining table went up in flames.

Mrs. Bates continued to reminisce. The Duchess had named the dog after her late husband. He was a lumbering, clumsy oaf too. Had a habit of falling over a lot, causing accidents. Mind you, that was the drink. Paralytic at all times of the day or night the old Duke had been. Very similar to Sir Montague Pugh in that respect.

He had always enjoyed a good dinner party, though. Wonder what he'd have made of the last one! Probably laughing his head off at the shenanigans, wherever he was now.

'You couldn't write it,' he always used to say about life and its dramas. 'You just couldn't write it.' 'Well,' Mrs. Bates mused to herself. 'P'rhaps one day when I 'as the time, I might 'ave a go. You never know; I just might at that'.

Daydreaming as she stood at the sink, up to her elbows in soapsuds, the plump cook began to think out loud. She smiled secretively to herself. Yes, that was how she would begin her story, it was perfect.

The Dowager Duchess took her place at the head of the table and bowed graciously to her guests . . .'